THE DUKE'S PREDICAMENT

1811. Lady Sarah and Paul March-
and marry as planned — but when
the garden party to celebrate their
nuptials is ruined by an unpleasant
incident, the Duke of Denchester
is faced with a predicament. Mean-
while, governess Hannah Westley has
a predicament of her own: should
she marry steady, reliable Doctor
Peterson — or follow the drum with
soldier Patrick O'Riley? Hannah
decides to follow Patrick to Portugal;
but when he chooses his career over
their happiness, she returns to England . . .

FENELLA J. MILLER

THE DUKE'S PREDICAMENT

Complete and Unabridged

LINFORD
Leicester

First published in Great Britain in 2020

First Linford Edition
published 2022

*A catalogue record for this book is available
from the British Library.*

ISBN 978-1-4448-4823-6

1

Radley Manor, July 1811.

Amanda was revelling in her new position as the Duchess of Denchester, not because she was now elevated above most others in the country but because she was Richard's beloved wife. She stood beside him looking out over the grounds of the Manor now almost unrecognisable with the marquees, trestles, bunting, flags and balloons put out for the garden party and the celebration of her sister's wedding to Paul.

'It's hard to credit that there's to be a second wedding here and so soon after ours. I just wish Mama thought herself well enough to attend and wasn't remaining in her apartment with the door locked.'

Richard pulled her closer. 'She's the best person to judge when her fits of mania are about to start. The way we've arranged things she'll be able to watch everything, apart from the ceremony itself, from her windows upstairs.'

'Have you noticed how both Doctor Peterson and Mr O'Riley are taking an interest in Miss Westley? It wouldn't surprise me to learn that Beth's governess will soon depart to be the wife of one or the other.'

'I might be a man, sweetheart, but I am aware of such things. I've been making enquiries and have the names of several young ladies who could replace her if that were to be the case. Mrs Marchand, Paul's mother, has proved to be a godsend. Having her here as companion to your mother has worked even better than I'd hoped.'

'We'll all be related to each other in some strange way. Paul will become my brother-in-law and when my sister becomes his wife, she will be daughter to Mrs Marchand.'

'At least if Miss Westley marries either Patrick or the doctor then she'll not be making her home under this roof. Have you any preference as to which one she should choose?'

'I like both gentlemen and it's clear that she's torn between them. Let's hope they don't come to blows as I doubt that the doctor would be any match for Patrick. Being an ex-sergeant major makes him tougher and he's certainly broader and taller.'

A flash of blue behind the largest marquee attracted her attention. It was Beth, her youngest sibling, and she'd escaped from Miss Westley again. Richard laughed and vaulted over the balustrade.

'I'll fetch her back, darling, why don't you return to our apartment and change into your wedding finery? I'll join you shortly.'

He ran easily, like the athletic gentleman he was, and she couldn't take her eyes from him. How had she been so lucky as to marry him when he could have had anyone in the country for his bride? She didn't doubt that he loved her, but sometimes he was distracted in her company as if he might possibly be regretting his choice.

On her way to her apartment she walked around the reception rooms one final time and was satisfied that everything was in place. The flower arrangements were perfect, not too formal, and the overwhelming scent of roses filled every chamber.

She and Richard had been married in the family chapel a few weeks ago and although they had been intimate every night her monthly courses had still arrived on time — twice. Was it this that was causing her beloved husband to regret his decision? There was no one she could ask about such a delicate matter apart from perhaps Mrs Marchand, but she was no longer joining them downstairs since Mama was unwell again.

Another constant worry were the changes she'd noticed in her younger sister — Dr Peterson had warned them that although Beth had the mental capacity of a small child, she was physically a woman and might well experience an interest in young gentlemen.

The arrival of the three puppies had been a temporary distraction but every day now Beth evaded her governess and went in search of more interesting activities. Richard with a mixture of love and firmness was the only one able to persuade her sibling to behave appropriately.

Obviously, there could be no happy outcome as Beth could never marry. She was a beautiful girl, an heiress, an aristocrat, but so damaged mentally being a wife and mother was out of the question. Richard had suggested appointing two bodyguards to escort her wherever she went. These would be as much to warn off potential predators as for Beth's safety.

It was fortunate indeed that her sister didn't go into company, remained safe at Radley Manor, but these past few days there'd been a constant toing and froing of workmen and naturally some of these were young men. There was no danger that anyone working for the family would take advantage of the situation but the more time Beth spent chasing after any young man the more likely it was that she could be enticed away by someone less scrupulous.

The wedding ceremony was to be held in the ballroom as a special licence had been obtained. Sarah hadn't wished to replicate her sister's wedding by using the family chapel for a second time. New accommodations had been prepared for Sarah and her soon-to-be husband, Paul, and these were on the other side of the house so they could have their privacy.

They could dine with the family but had their own reception rooms and personal staff so could remain apart if that's what they desired. The happy couple were to leave after the garden party and ball for an extended wedding trip to the Lake District. She and Richard had only had two nights in his hunting lodge in Norfolk before he was called away to rescue Patrick who had been wrongly arrested as a deserter.

Would he suggest they returned there and complete their honeymoon when the wedding was over? They scarcely had time to speak to each other during the day and at night there was little talking involved in their activities. Making love — as he had called this highly enjoyable activity — was something she eagerly anticipated but she did miss being able to spend time with him without the passion.

He was a duke, he had massive responsibilities to those in his demesne, to his family, to his many estates and businesses. Therefore, talking to his wife must appear of less importance than these other matters. She also had plenty to do. She was running a large household but it just wasn't enough for her. Before their marriage — before his arrival last year — everything had been her concern and she missed being involved with the decision-making, the finances and so on.

Richard was to be groomsman for Paul, so again he was more concerned in the wedding than she was. This time there were to be two dozen guests to witness the ceremony, an elaborate wedding breakfast would be served afterwards in the largest marquee, and then the grounds would be open to the villagers and neighbours for the garden party. After that there would be a ball indoors for their neighbours and family.

Originally these had been planned to celebrate her wedding but now they were solely for Sarah and Paul. She didn't resent this in any way as she loved her sister dearly but . . . but. No time for repining. Today was a celebration for her sister and her new brother. If only her own night-time activity would result in a pregnancy, she would be content.

★ ★ ★

'Miss Westley, Miss Westley, why did I have to come in? I like it out there talking to the men getting things ready for the wedding.'

'Beth, his grace explained it to you. Young ladies do not go out and speak to workmen. It's just not acceptable behaviour,' Hannah said as she set out the watercolours hoping this would occupy her charge until it was time to change for the ceremony.

'I want to get married like Sarah and Amanda. Are you going to get married? Are you going to marry Doctor Peterson or Mr O'Riley?'

'I'm not intending to marry anybody and I've certainly had no offers from either of those gentlemen.'

'Will they be here today? I prefer Mr O'Riley — if you don't want to marry him do you think he will marry me instead?'

The duke overheard this last remark and exchanged a worried glance with her.

'Nobody is going to marry you, sweetheart, don't you remember we talked about this? You've got your puppy to look after and when there are babies you will be needed to help with them.'

'I don't like dogs anymore. My puppy, Marigold, bit me and made my finger bleed. Silly Billy, Sarah's puppy, tore my skirt and your Mouse doesn't speak to me at all.'

'I see that you're going to paint — are you going to paint that vase of summer flowers on the table?'

Beth pulled a face. 'I don't like flowers, they smell horrible.'

'Why don't you paint a picture for your grandmama of the exciting things outside in the grounds? Did you know that I've arranged for an air balloon to visit? If you behave yourself I might allow you to go up in it.'

Lady Beth's expression changed to sunny. 'I am good, I am very good today. I'll paint a lovely picture for Grandmama and then may I put on my new gown for the wedding?'

'As soon as you've finished your painting, you must wash your face and hands and then Jenny will help you dress. Remember, you may have your hair put up today in a grown-up style. Isn't that exciting?'

The duke smiled his thanks and walked away. Hannah was concerened Beth's chatter about Patrick and the doctor had been overheard. If the girl had

10

noticed the attention she was receiving from both of them then she was certain her employers must also have observed the same thing.

Her cheeks flushed, not from pleasure but from embarrassment. It was flattering to have two personable gentlemen showing an interest but neither of them was of any consequence to her. If she ever married — which was highly unlikely — it would be to someone who could not only provide for her, who had a modest estate, an income not dependent on an employer's whim, but a gentleman she could love.

Patrick O'Riley was a good friend, she'd known him for more than a year, and he was certainly a handsome man, and just being with him made her heart beat a little faster. He was intelligent and kind, but if she married him, they would be forever tied to this family, and that wouldn't be something she'd enjoy.

Also, he was a soldier to his core despite having retired from the army. The thought of sharing her bed with a man who'd killed for his living was abhorrent to her. Another count against him was the fact that he could still be arrested and forced to sign on for a further five years. That possibility loomed large in her thoughts.

Doctor Peterson, on the other hand, was wealthy, had all the attributes she desired but for some reason he didn't stir her senses in the same way that Patrick did. He wasn't exactly handsome, but he was well-set-up, an excellent physician, and she knew if she gave him the slightest encouragement he would likely make her an offer.

It was a conundrum and having Beth prattle on about both gentlemen didn't help one jot. She must put this personal problem aside and concentrate on her duties. Her charge was as beautiful as her sister Sarah, with corn-coloured hair and bright blue eyes, and if one didn't know she was impaired one would think she was a normal young lady.

There had been an incident in London when an unscrupulous fortune hunter had mistaken her for her sister and his grace had been obliged to sort that out. Sarah's reputation had almost been ruined but more worryingly it had given Beth a taste for adult pastimes.

★ ★ ★

'That's a beautiful painting, Beth, shall we leave it on the easel to dry and then we'll get someone to frame it? It deserves to be on the wall. Why not give it to Lady Sarah and Mr Marchand as a wedding gift?'

The girl clapped her hands. 'I will, I will. Now, Miss Westley, is it time to change into my new gown?'

'It is indeed, my dear. Look, your maid has come to collect you and help you dress. I must also do the same. I'm so looking forward to seeing Lady Sarah married and then we have the added excitement of a garden party.'

They no longer referred to the two girls who took care of Beth's personal needs as nursemaids, although that's what they were. Everything was being done that was feasible in order to treat her like an adult and not a six-year-old.

Hannah didn't have a personal maid although she did have a chambermaid assigned to her. Therefore, she tended to herself. Not that she had a large wardrobe to select from — after all she was little more than a well-educated servant — but she did have a new gown that she'd sewn herself for this event and an evening gown for tonight.

Her hair remained as it always was, a neat arrangement at the nape of her neck. However, as she had abundant curls a few of these were allowed to frame her face. Her gown was pale green with an emerald green sash and bugle beads around the neckline. Her best bonnet had been relined in matching material and the ribbons replaced with the same emerald green of her sash.

As she was going to be tramping about outside she put on her boots which fortunately would be invisible beneath the hem of her dress. She checked that her reticule had handkerchiefs, a purse with some coins, some barley sugar twists and her fan, and then was ready to depart.

Her chamber was on the same floor as Beth's, the nursery floor, but it was a spacious room with its own sitting room and had a lovely view of the gardens. As she stepped out her charge also appeared looking charming in her sprigged muslin, her glorious golden curls neatly arranged and topped with a new chip straw bonnet.

'You look pretty, Miss Westley. I've not seen that gown before.'

'Thank you for saying so, Beth, I appreciate the compliment. And you look lovely in your new ensemble. Are you going to take the matching parasol as it's going to be hot in the gardens this afternoon?'

'I don't like it, nasty, pokey thing. Will you carry it for me and hold it if I get hot?'

'No, a young lady takes care of these things herself. If you wish to leave it behind then so be it. Remember to hold up your skirts so you don't tear the hem as we go downstairs.'

Beth was usually dressed in mid-calf length dresses with a pinafore as this was easier for her to manage. Only on special occasions did she appear as she was. Obviously, all the staff were aware of the girl's limitations, but there would be guests at the wedding breakfast and the garden party who could mistake her for an ordinary young lady and this was could be where the problems could start. She must be extra vigilant today.

★ ★ ★

Patrick had been sharing the Dower House with the bridegroom, but from today Paul would become one of the family and above his touch. There was less dust on every surface nowadays from the building works going on a few hundred yards away. Things had improved now the roof was on the new house for his grace and his wife. The building wouldn't be completed for another year.

'Patrick, how do I look? Hopefully not as terrified as I feel,' Paul said as he made the final touches to his elaborate neckcloth.

'Think of it as going into a battle, my friend, chin up and shoulders back.'

'That advice might be valuable if I'd had the experience that you have. As you very well know I resigned my commission before being involved in any fighting. Which reminds me, isn't it about time you heard from Horse Guards?'

'They're not famous for their speedy decision-making. Your ensign will have reached Portugal and delivered the letters by now so I'm hopeful things will finally be resolved.'

Even to himself he sounded different nowadays — in order to pretend to be a gentleman he'd ironed out the Irish brogue, the profanities and cant that he'd used as a sergeant major, and now spoke like everyone else, but he hadn't changed inside.

He'd spent years wearing just his red-coat, and sometimes when he caught a glimpse of himself in a glass he scarcely recognised the fellow he'd become. The walnut juice he'd been dying his hair with had now gone and now his fiery red hair looked exactly the same as it had always done.

'The carriage has arrived. We'd better go, the groom should always be there in advance of the bride, even I know that.'

'I've enjoyed living here with you, Patrick, and it's going to be strange being part of the Denchester family.'

'You're a toff, one of them, Paul, it comes naturally for you.'

It was three miles to Radley Manor and he decided then that he would walk home when the wedding celebrations were over. He'd never ridden in a carriage by himself — he wasn't a gentleman born and bred — and didn't want to ape his betters. He chuckled at the absurdity of his thoughts as he would have to return to change into his evening rig for the ball tonight.

The ballroom was decked out in flowers, banners and ribbons and there were rows of chairs facing a lectern at the front. There was an aisle between them through which the bride would walk on the arm of the duke and return beside her new husband.

There was an orchestra tuning up at the back of the room and no doubt this would be playing for couples to dance at the ball this evening. He was hoping to claim Miss Westley for two dances. He scowled. That damned doctor would no doubt be hoping to do the same.

He must put his wishes aside as he couldn't offer her the kind of life she deserved. She would be better off as a doctor's wife living in her own grand house — something he could never give her. He wasn't a sentimental sort of man but, since he'd met her last year, he'd viewed things differently. If he was honest with himself, he knew he'd pushed his Irish roots aside in order to impress her.

The duke, he believed he could no longer refer to him as *major* as he'd done initially, was waiting to greet them looking every inch an aristocrat. It was hard to credit that two years ago they'd been fighting side by side in Portugal, both career soldiers, neither of them anticipating how their lives would change.

'Are you ready, Paul, still time to change your mind,' the duke said in jest.

'No, sir, I'm eager to say my vows. I can't tell you what a difference it makes having my mother living under the same roof and knowing that she's happy again.'

'Mrs Marchand has made an enormous difference to our lives. Amanda and I are delighted to have her as part of the family. See — the ladies are arriving now.' He laughed. 'Don't look so terrified, not your bride. I'm to fetch her when everyone else is seated.'

Patrick turned. His eyes widened. Hannah looked quite stunning, every inch a lady, and so far out of his reach he accepted at last that it wasn't to be. Then he grinned. All the ladies were wearing bonnets which looked decidedly odd when they were indoors.

'Mr O'Riley, what has amused you about our arrival?' Miss Westley said.

He pointed to her hat and she returned his smile. 'I know, ridiculous, but as the wedding breakfast is to be served in the marquee, which is technically outside, bonnets are *de rigueur*.'

'Lady Elizabeth, might I be permitted to compliment you on your gown?'

He'd expected her to clap, to spin around demonstrating how the skirts swirled about her ankles, but to his surprise she nodded and smiled as any girl would do.

'Thank you, Mr O'Riley. I think that Miss Westley's gown is pretty too, don't you?'

'It is, my lady, I'm honoured to be in your company.'

The orchestra began to play something he recognised as Bach and he stepped aside to allow Paul to greet his mother.

2

Amanda stood beside Richard and watched her sister marry a man she'd only known a few weeks. This didn't bother her as it was obvious to everyone how much in love they were. He seemed to sense she was thinking about him and reached out and took her hand in his. He squeezed it gently and spoke softly into her ear.

'I have to sign the register, darling, but then I'll not leave your side again today. I love you and know you feel neglected. Things will improve once this is out of the way.'

'I love you too and if Sarah and Paul are half as happy as we are then they'll be doing very well.'

He touched her face with his hand and then strode off to the table set out for the purpose. Upon this the register and marriage certificate could be filled in and witnessed correctly.

The orchestra were playing Bach again, a favourite composer of hers. Beth was fidgeting at her side. 'It won't be much longer, sweetheart, then we'll all be going outside to the big marquee and a delicious wedding breakfast will be served.'

'Why is it called breakfast when it's in the afternoon, Amanda?'

'I don't really know. But then when we go out to visit in the afternoon it's called a morning call, isn't it?'

'It is, and I think that's very silly too.'

There was a sudden scuffle at the back of the room which attracted their attention. Ladies were protesting, gentlemen standing up. What on earth was going on?

Suddenly an unfortunate cat shot between her feet followed by three small shaggy dogs. The racket attracted the attention of the small group around the table. Patrick, Richard and Paul turned first and reacted immediately as one would expect from ex-soldiers.

If they'd discussed who should collect

which puppy, she certainly didn't hear it but they split up and, in seconds, the furore was over. Richard held up Mouse, Patrick had Marigold and Paul collected Silly Billy. The cat vanished over the windowsill much to the relief of everyone present. The three gentlemen in their smart clothes marched one behind the other down the aisle and vanished. Sarah was left standing at the altar with her mother-in-law.

Beth was giggling so much Amanda feared her sister would fall from her chair. She left Miss Westley to deal with this and rushed over to Sarah. 'Well, that was exciting and unusual. Shall we march down the aisle one behind the other as the gentlemen did?'

Sarah was laughing almost as much as Beth. 'Oh yes, let's do that. I've never seen anything so funny in my life and it's the perfect start to my marriage. I wonder how the dogs got out?'

The orchestra had continued playing as if nothing untoward had occurred and now the guests were seated again and most of them were laughing too. Amanda caught the eye of the conductor and he understood immediately.

The orchestra struck up a martial tune ideal for marching down the aisle. Sarah set off, Amanda followed her, then Beth jumped to her feet and came third. Mrs Marchand and Miss Westley followed along behind. What the guests thought of this bizarre spectacle she'd no idea and cared less.

They were all in the entrance hall when the gentlemen returned. Sarah ran into the arms of her husband and he picked up and kissed her thoroughly. She did the same and Richard didn't fail her. She had no time to see what Patrick did with Miss Westley but when Richard finally released her, they were standing very close together looking rather pleased with themselves. Mrs Marchand was no longer there — no doubt she'd returned to her duties with Mama. The only one not looking happy was Beth. However, Miss Westley immediately took charge of the situation and averted a possible incident.

'Should we tell the other guests the ceremony is over and they should make their way to the marquee?'

Sarah answered the question she'd directed at Richard. 'They'll soon realise when we don't go back in. I feel sorry for the vicar he must think we've all run mad.'

She and Paul linked arms and dashed off through the drawing room and out of the open French doors. The rest of them followed on. Richard had offered to lay a carpet across the grass but both she and Sarah had insisted this was unnecessary.

She stepped into the tent and paused to admire what had been achieved. 'Isn't this absolutely splendid? So much better than being squashed together inside. It was an inspired suggestion to arrange things this way as now the villagers and staff can enjoy their own dance out here whilst we're attending our far more formal, and less enjoyable, ball inside.'

'As the owners of all this magnificence, sweetheart, it behoves us to attend both events. From the racket behind us I think our guests are coming to join us so we'd better take our seats.'

* * *

The wedding breakfast was sumptuous, champagne and various wines were served with each course, but she wisely stuck to lemonade. Alcohol didn't agree with her.

Eventually the meal was over and Paul stood up. He tapped his glass and everyone fell silent. 'I wish to thank you for coming and apologise for the minor interruption by the puppies and the cat. As you can hear the garden party is about to start. There will be fire-eaters, stilt-walkers, fortune tellers as well as a coconut shy and a tug of war. But, the most exciting event will be the air balloon. I can't wait to ascend in it. My wife and I are going out to enjoy the delights. I hope you will join us.'

There was a spontaneous round of applause and the scrape of chairs being pushed back on the board floor that had been laid inside the marquee.

'I think there's going to be trouble with Beth this afternoon, Richard. From her cheeks I'd say she's been drinking wine whilst Miss Westley was distracted. I think we'd better escort her, she'll not misbehave if we're with her.'

'I'd hoped to spend the time alone with you — well, as alone as we ever are nowadays. Miss Westley, as far as I recall, hasn't taken a day off since she arrived last year. Excuse me, my love, I'm going to collect Beth and tell her governess that she can have the remainder of the day and tomorrow as much deserved, and belated, free time.'

'Doctor Peterson was to attend the wedding itself but he isn't here. I don't recall having received a cancellation from him. I suppose he must have been called away to an emergency.' She put her hand through his arm and they moved swiftly towards Beth and Miss Westley.

Her sister was trying to pull away from her governess. There was going to be an unpleasant scene at any moment. Richard moved so swiftly she was forced to release his arm. Then he was beside Beth.

'You will not make a scene, young lady. Either you behave yourself or I'm taking you up to your room and you shall remain there and miss all the excitement here.'

'I won't go in. I don't like you.'

He tightened his hold and spoke softly to the truculent girl. 'Then I'm afraid it's inside for you.' He whisked her away before she could protest and anyone notice the altercation.

'Miss Westley, there's no need for you to go with my sister. You must have the remainder of the day to yourself and his grace suggests you take tomorrow as well.'

'I should be with her. She's my responsibility . . .'

'Not today or tomorrow — Nanny and the nursemaids are quite capable of looking after her. Excuse me, I must go and see her settled. You enjoy yourself. I'll expect to see you at the ball tonight.'

Hannah was torn by the pull of her duty towards her charge and the thought that she could enjoy the delights available today without responsibility.

Patrick had watched the drama and now offered his arm. 'You deserve some time off, Miss Westley. I'm determined to go up in the balloon and am hoping I can entice you to join me.'

'I'm not sure I wish to do so but I'm intrigued. I understand that it's filled with some sort of gas and is being inflated at this very moment.'

'Then that's what we shall do first. I'm yours to command for the remainder of the day. I, too, have been given two days' furlough. Perhaps you might consider accompanying me for a picnic or some such nonsense tomorrow?'

She smiled up at him. 'What I would like to do is go for a gentle hack about the countryside. I'm a novice rider and since Beth has once more taken against horses for some reason, I no longer have the opportunity to go out with her.'

They threaded their way through the growing crowd of happy tenants, employees and villagers accompanied by their families. It wasn't often the two sides mixed so freely. Mind you, the Denchester family were like no other of their status. His grace, having grown up with no expectation of becoming the duke, had been a career soldier like Patrick, so had not become arrogant and treated everyone with respect from the lowliest bootboy to a visiting aristocrat.

From his superior height her escort was able to see in which direction to go. 'It's already half-full and attracting a deal of attention. I think it will be the main attraction, don't you?'

'Imagine the disappointment if the weather had turned and it was raining and not glorious summer sunshine.' Talking about the weather was a safe topic but what she really wanted to do was discuss the brief moment in the entrance hall when he had raised her hand and kissed her knuckles. It was the lightest of kisses and probably meant nothing at all — but she was certain Beth had witnessed it and this was why she'd become disobedient and difficult.

Then all thought of this troubling incident fled from her mind when she saw the top of the balloon billowing above the heads of the gawping crowd.

'Oh, my goodness! I'd no idea it would be so enormous. What's that alarming hissing sound I can hear?'

Instinctively she moved closer to him and he didn't move away. But neither did he take her hand or put his arm around her in a way that might have been construed as taking liberties.

'Look, over there are barrels of gas and what you hear is the gas going into the balloon. The basket is pegged to the ground with those iron loops and the hessian bags hanging over the side will be dropped in order for the balloon to rise higher.'

There were half a dozen men busy around the rapidly inflating balloon but two of them, better dressed than the others, must be the aeronauts.

'How do you know so much about this? Do you have secret yearnings to be an aeronaut yourself?'

He grinned and shook his head. 'I'm quite happy to go up as long as it's firmly tethered to the earth. I'd not wish to be at the mercy of the wind and not know in which direction I'd be taken.'

'I imagine rising is safe enough but landing might well be problematical — certainly not something I'd wish to experience.'

A pretty young woman brightly dressed in stripes, her wild brown hair haphazardly piled on top of her head, approached them. 'Do you wish to put your names down, ma'am, sir? There are already a dozen people ahead of you.'

'Yes, we do wish to ascend. Mr O'Riley is my name. When should we return here?'

'The balloon will be ready in half an hour. The weather's perfect, no wind at all. If you would care to return in two hours it should be your turn by then.'

She pointed at Hannah's gown. 'It's a mite chilly up there, ma'am, so you might want to put on a cloak for your ascent.'

Patrick handed over the required coins and they moved aside to allow other eager would-be aeronauts to sign up for the experience.

'There's so much to see, shall we start from here and make a complete circuit? There are numerous stalls and side-shows — it's better than any country fair I've ever attended.'

He held out his arm and willingly she slipped her hand through it. She felt a moment's guilt that she wasn't upstairs with Beth, but then pushed it aside. Although she had one afternoon a week to herself, she'd not taken any more time away from her charge than that.

The two hours sped by as there was so much to see and her companion kept her amused with his lively wit and obvious enjoyment of all that was on offer. The balloon had floated up many times much to the enjoyment of the watching crowd and now she was confident it held no risk so was looking forward to her turn.

'I must go in and fetch my cloak, Patrick. Shall I meet you at the balloon in a quarter of an hour?'

'I'll be waiting. Are you still sure you wish to participate in this?'

She pointed into the sky where the balloon was floating and the occupants waving and gesticulating from within the basket. 'I can't wait, it's an opportunity to experience something unusual and I doubt it will occur again.'

As her small apartment was adjacent to the schoolroom and Beth's accommodation, she feared she might be unable to escape again. Perhaps it would have been better to send a maid to fetch her cloak and thus avoid the possibility.

Too late to repine — she must find it for herself and pray that Beth didn't notice her slipping in and out. The nursery floor was quiet and she began to breathe more easily. She collected the garment she needed then looked into the schoolroom. There was no sign of

Nanny and the two nursemaids were busy doing mending and looked up on her entry.

'Is Lady Beth resting?'

Both girls jumped up and curtsied briefly. 'She is, Miss Westley. After his grace spoke most sternly to her she settled down and played with her dolls. She asked if she could go to her bedchamber for a rest and we've not heard a peep from her since then.'

'I'll just look in on her before I go down again.' Hannah tiptoed to the door, which was ajar, and looked around. Her stomach turned over. The bed was empty — the room deserted — Beth had somehow tricked her watchers and was now God knows where.

★ ★ ★

Patrick watched Hannah move smoothly through the crowd, stopping to speak to many of the happy folk with that easy manner that she had. His good intentions had vanished when Peterson had failed to appear. It behoved him to escort her as he could hardly allow her to wander about unattended.

After the nonsense at the ceremony with the puppies and the cat he'd returned with his grace and Paul and been swept up in the moment. When the other two couples had kissed each other so fiercely he couldn't resist entrapping her hand and placing a light kiss on her knuckles.

Her cheeks had turned pink but she hadn't objected. Was it possible that she returned his feelings? That she was prepared to forego a life of luxury and ease and marry him?

There was no need to head towards the balloon just yet, he would wander about and then, when he spied her coming back, would walk with her rather than meet her there. He wandered to the far edge of the lawns where there were the caravans and small tents belonging to the Romany who had provided much of the entertainment.

It was quieter here, fewer people, and the trees that edged the grass cast a welcome shade. As he was passing a striped booth he saw Lady Beth vanish behind it accompanied by a well-dressed young gentleman that he didn't recognise.

How the hell had she managed to be out on her own? He followed the two of them and she was being led away and obviously not an unwilling companion to this bastard. He didn't hesitate. He grabbed the cove by his shoulder, spun him round and floored him with a massive right hook to the side of his jaw. Before the girl could protest, he picked her up and made a dash for the trees where her screams of protest wouldn't be heard.

He took off at the double and didn't pause despite her frantic kicks until they were far enough away to be safe from any spectators. He dumped her unceremoniously on her feet but kept a firm hold on her arms.

'Enough of that racket, my lady, I'm quite prepared to put you across my knee if you don't stop.' He had no intention of doing so but the threat was enough to calm her down. Her bonnet was on sideways, her gown creased and what looked suspiciously like grass stains across the back.

Her defiance crumpled and she burst into tears. He gathered her close and comforted her as he'd done many times before. She was, after all, still a child and couldn't be blamed for what had taken place.

'There, no need to cry, little one, you're safe now. Here, dry your eyes, and then you can hold my hand and I'll take you back.'

'I wanted to come out and see everything but Cousin Richard said I couldn't because I'd been a naughty girl. I pretended to be asleep and then slipped out.'

'Then the sooner we get you safely inside, my lady, the better. Are you ready?'

There was a path through the woods that avoided the garden party and hand in hand they walked back and she was entranced by the birds they saw, by the flowers, and insisted on picking a bunch to give to Hannah.

The enormity of her actions was beyond her — but God knows what his grace would do when he heard. He wanted to ask her if she'd been hurt but thought it not his business to make any more enquiries. Her grace or Hannah would be the best people to discuss something so intimate and delicate.

It was hard to keep smiling and chatting as if there was nothing wrong, as if he wasn't so angry he wanted to go back and break the neck of the man he'd knocked out. If this sweet child had been violated then the perpetrator would die whoever he might be. Patrick was quite prepared to swing at the end of a rope in order to see justice done.

3

Hannah didn't wait to reprimand the two girls for being so lax in their duties but ran down the stairs and out onto the terrace in the hope that she might spot Beth from this vantage point. The girl was wearing a pretty pink gown which should be easy to see amongst the drab colours of the less well-off.

At the very far side of the lawn by the trees she saw Patrick suddenly run full pelt and vanish behind one of the Romany tents. A few seconds later he appeared with Beth in his arms and headed for the woods.

She scanned the crowd and saw his grace not far away. She would speak to him immediately and then meet Patrick and Beth. She had a very bad feeling about what she'd seen.

The duke saw her approaching, abandoned his conversation and strode towards her. 'What's wrong? Is it Beth?'

Quickly she explained her anxiety. 'We'll go together, Miss Westley, and then I'll send word for my wife to join us inside.' From the grimness of his expression he feared the worst, as did she.

They exited via the side door that led to the stables and from there they could reach the woods without being observed by anyone. She unclipped her cloak and had it ready to envelop Beth when they reached her.

They stopped their headlong rush when they could hear voices approaching. Beth was chattering and laughing as if nothing was wrong, and Patrick answering. She exchanged a worried glance with the duke and he nodded when she showed him the cloak.

Beth was so busy examining the treasures she'd picked up along the way that she didn't notice their approach, however, Patrick did. He shook his head and her heart sank to her boots.

'Well, sweetheart, I'm disappointed in you. I thought you promised to remain inside and that I would come and get you in time for your balloon ride.'

'Cousin Richard, I decided I wouldn't wait for you. I met a nice gentleman and he showed me lots of interesting things we could do to pass the time. Then Mr O'Riley knocked him out and made me come with him.' She stamped her foot and glared at them. 'He threatened to spank me. I want you to send him away right now.' Regaling this tale brought back Beth's indignation and she turned and kicked poor Patrick in the shins.

There were grass stains on the back of her gown and there could only be one way they had got there. Whatever had happened to Beth, and Hannah feared it was appalling, the girl wasn't to be allowed to behave so badly. The duke was having none of this nonsense.

'He was right to threaten to chastise you. I'm tempted to do the same myself. Are you going to walk with me like a sensible young lady or do I have to carry you like a baby?'

His stern tone was enough to stem the threatened tantrum. 'I'll come like a good girl. Miss Westley, will you hold my hand? Cousin Richard and Mr O'Riley are very cross with me.'

The duke nodded his agreement. He spoke quietly to her so Beth couldn't overhear. 'Patrick and I are going to find this person and put him somewhere he can't communicate with others until we know exactly what took place. I'll have Amanda join you upstairs.'

'Yes, your grace, I'll do that. Come along, sweetheart, let's hurry, but first I'm going to put my nice cloak around you so no one can see the nasty marks you have on your pretty dress.'

The girl didn't object and put her hand trustingly in hers. 'I don't like it when gentlemen are cross with me. I don't mean to be naughty; I want to be a good girl all the time in future.'

'I'm glad to hear it. Now, tell me about these lovely things you've picked. Do you know the names of all these flowers?'

They took the back staircase and went straight to the nursery. Nanny and the two nursemaids were waiting anxiously.

Hannah wasn't sure having them over-hear any subsequent conversations was a good idea because neither of the nurse-maids could be trusted to keep a secret to themselves. The problem was solved for her when her grace stalked in.

'You three are dismissed from my service. You will go to your rooms and remain there until arrangements can be made for you to depart. His grace will decide whether you are to be given a reference or not.'

The two maids burst into noisy tears but Nanny was made of sterner stuff and understood this was no more than they deserved. They had all been derelict in their duties.

She curtsied to her grace. 'I apologise, your grace, it was my fault. I'm in charge of the nursery floor and I went outside to see the hot air balloon, leaving the two girls alone.'

'I'm not interested in excuses, Nanny. Lady Elizabeth was in your care, we trusted you to keep her safe and you have failed us.'

The three trooped miserably away and then Beth started to scream. Perhaps it hadn't been such a good idea to hold this conversation in front of her when she was already so fragile. The noise echoed and Hannah was sure it could be heard outside through the open windows.

Mrs Marchand at that moment rushed in closing the door behind her and then dashed around the room banging shut the windows.

'Beth, darling, you mustn't make that noise. It will give you the most fearful headache and you might well cast up your accounts. Come now, let's take you into your bedroom and we can get you fresh and clean.'

Between the two of them they persuaded the distraught girl into her room and she then collapsed onto the bed. Hannah climbed on beside her and rocked her in her arms until finally Beth sobbed herself to sleep and she was able to rejoin the other two who had been watching anxiously from the door.

'Your grace, forgive me, but I think we

should send for Doctor Peterson. There was a gentleman involved.'

The duchess blanched as the meaning behind these words were realised. 'I think I saw him arrive a while ago. I'll stay here and watch Beth; you go and find him.'

'His grace and Mr O'Riley are dealing with the gentleman concerned and will be with you once that has been accomplished.'

'I understand. We must do our best not to let Sarah or Paul hear of this disaster. We cannot cancel the ball either at this late date as half the guests are already here enjoying the garden party.'

'I am available and can remain with Lady Elizabeth and Miss Westley. Your mama has taken a sleeping draught and won't wake until the morning. She has her dresser and another maid sitting with her,' Mrs Marchand said.

'Thank you, ma'am, your assistance will be invaluable. Richard and I must be at the ball or there will be gossip and we wish to avoid that at all costs. Heaven knows how many people saw my poor sister go off with that man — for all we know word has spread already.'

Hannah couldn't keep back her biggest worry. 'Whatever the monster did, I pray that his grace and Mr O'Riley don't murder him.'

His grace spoke from behind them. 'He's trussed up like a Christmas goose and locked in an outhouse. Patrick's blow rendered him unconscious but it also broke his jaw. Little point in trying to interrogate him as he's unable to speak coherently. Peterson is attending to him now and will then come immediately upstairs.'

★ ★ ★

Patrick waited with the doctor whilst he examined the man he'd injured. The molester was semi-conscious and moaning a lot, and in no fit state to be questioned. On closer examination of the villain's clothes there was no doubt that he was not a villager, but as his cuffs were worn, his boots also, this indicated he wasn't from a wealthy family either.

Peterson stepped back after fastening the bandage he'd put around the man's chin to hold his jaw in place. 'He'll have to drink soup for the next few weeks. Is it absolutely necessary that he's tied up? He would do better in bed.'

'He assaulted Lady Elizabeth. We fear the worst and you're needed upstairs to examine her.'

The doctor's expression changed to one of loathing and he stepped away without another glance. 'Is he known to you? Let's hope he's not the son of someone important as if he did violate the duke's ward then I doubt he'll leave here alive.'

'I'll dispose of him. There's no need for anyone else to be involved. I don't give a damn who his parents are. He's on borrowed time.'

The sounds from those enjoying the garden party did nothing to lift his spirits. He should have been ascending in the balloon with Hannah — but everything had changed now. He must distance himself from her, push her towards the doctor, as he could see his days of freedom were numbered.

It occurred to him that it might be sensible to dispatch the bastard in the outhouse immediately and then head for the coast and re-enlist as soon as he got to Portugal. That way there'd be no unpleasantness attached to the family and he'd still be alive.

Peterson grabbed his elbow. 'No, my friend, now is not the time. His grace will wish to speak to you before you do anything precipitous.'

With some reluctance he nodded and together they entered the house and made their stealthy way upstairs. God knows how such a delicate thing as the examination of little Beth was going to be managed. He doubted it could be accomplished without upsetting her further.

When they reached the first floor, upon which were the guest and family rooms, the duke was waiting for them. 'We need to talk, not upstairs, come into my apartment where we can be private.'

None of them spoke until they were safely inside and the door closed. 'Beth's sleeping and the ladies are with her. Those that should have taken care of her have been dismissed and will leave here tomorrow. What about the perpetrator of this atrocity?'

Peterson explained the situation and the duke listened attentively. 'Patrick, I need you to find out who he is. From your description he's unlikely to be the son of anyone we know personally. He could be a hanger-on, someone who came with a more important family. I can't make a decision on his future until I know his provenance.'

'I'll get onto it immediately. I'll also talk to as many guests as possible to see if what happened is already common knowledge. I'll start with the Romany camp. I didn't see anyone, but there's probably an old crone in one of the caravans who saw everything.'

'We'll reconvene here in an hour. Good hunting, my friend.' He turned to the doctor. 'Your services won't be required until my sister awakes. There's no need to upset her more than necessary.'

It seemed wrong to be wandering about surrounded by such jollity, smiling and nodding, when something so dreadful had happened. He spoke to a dozen or more, both the well-to-do and the local villagers, and he was certain nobody had seen Beth with that rogue.

He could hardly ask directly after the bastard without drawing attention to the reason he might be enquiring but he was quite sure no one was looking for him. He'd moved slowly through the throng, even stopping to watch the balloon go up, and was now close enough to the caravans to move between them and find someone to speak to.

He had no luck at the first caravan but the door opened on the second and a stooped old man beckoned him in.

'I knows why you're here, it's about that young'un in the pink dress.'

'It is, sir, can you tell me what happened?'

'It ain't as bad as you think, that varmint had her on the grass but I set the dogs on him and he jumped up pretty quick. He were just taking her somewhere else when you shows up.'

'Thank God and thank you. Forgive me, I must take the good news to the duke and duchess. Believe me, he'll come and see you himself to give you his thanks when this is sorted.' He went to dip into his purse but the old man shook his head.

'Don't want yer gold, young sir, there's not many a place we is made as welcome as here.'

Patrick returned by the woodland path running flat out. The news he had would mean that the doctor wouldn't have to make an intrusive examination. Beth had suffered no more than a fright.

He thundered up the nursery staircase and found the duke gazing sombrely out of the window. 'She wasn't harmed, an old Romany set the dogs on her attacker and I arrived moments later. I offered him a reward but he refused.' The doctor wasn't there. 'I'm not too late to stop Peterson, am I?'

'Peterson is with Miss Westley in her sitting room. I'm indebted to you, my friend, this could have been so much worse. I don't suppose you discovered the identity of the culprit?'

'Unfortunately not, your grace. I'm certain he's not the son of anyone you know. As far as I could discover he's not been missed. I could hardly ask directly after him.'

'Why don't you tell Peterson the good news? I'll inform Amanda and Mrs Marchand who are sitting with Beth at the moment.'

'What do we do with the bugger in the shed, your grace? Obviously, he's in no position to gossip until his jaw is mended but after that he'll be free to blacken her name. Or, he could resort to blackmail.'

'One thing I'm quite certain of, Patrick, is that if you hadn't arrived when you did things would have been quite different.'

'You haven't answered my question,

sir. I thought I could dispose of him and then disappear — head for Portugal and re-enlist which would solve both problems.'

'I don't wish you to do either. This is my predicament and I'll solve it without endangering your life. I'll speak to Amanda before I make a decision.'

Patrick headed for Hannah's apartment eager to give her the good news. He was somewhat concerned that the quack was with her, but in the circumstances he couldn't object. It might very well be fortuitous and make his possible departure easier for him.

The door was wide open and they were sitting by the window a goodly distance between them. A rush of relief washed over him and his smile when he entered made his news redundant.

★ ★ ★

Amanda looked up when Richard came in. He was smiling and she rushed to him. 'There's no need for Peterson to

55

look at her. She was mauled but not violated.'

Mrs Marchand overheard his comment and dabbed her eyes. 'Then her recovery won't be as difficult. I'll be with her tonight — I'll sleep beside her. I'll fetch what I need if you would stay here until I return.'

'That's kind of you, ma'am, and much appreciated,' Richard said. 'I'm not sure any of us wish to attend the ball but for Sarah and Paul's sake we must do so. I've no wish for them to hear about this until tomorrow.'

'I'll not be long. Then, despite the circumstances, I think you should return to the garden party as people will be wondering what's happened to you all.'

'I would like to go up in the balloon, I've been watching it rising and falling from the window,' Amanda said.

'Then so you shall, my love. Patrick was going to take Miss Westley, but no doubt they've missed their slot. Before we participate in the various activities, I must speak to the old man who acted so promptly to save Beth.'

'First, I'll rescue my bonnet, heaven knows where I put it down in my rush to come up here. I should like to come with you and thank the old gentleman in person. Would that be acceptable?'

'I don't give a damn if it isn't, and neither should you. It's not like you to be so hesitant, sweetheart. Find your bonnet and I'll meet you on the terrace in a few minutes.'

The missing headwear was perched on a chair in the schoolroom. Fortunately, there was a mirror and she was able to restore it to its rightful place and be ready in moments. Miss Westley's apartment opened from the schoolroom and she could hear voices in there.

'Miss Westley, Mr O'Riley, Richard and I intend to take a turn in the balloon. As you missed your opportunity why don't you come with us. I'm quite certain we won't have to stand in line.'

Patrick appeared at the door. 'If you're quite sure, then we should love to join you.'

Only then did Amanda realise the doctor was also within the room and she'd not included him in the invitation. He didn't seem at all offended by this omission. He strolled out and smiled at her.

'I've no intention whatsoever of taking a ride in that monstrosity. If God had meant us to be airborne, he would have given us wings like the birds.'

She knew him to be jesting and laughed. 'In which case, you can stand and watch and admire our courage. We expected you earlier. No doubt you were called to an emergency which I hope was resolved satisfactorily.'

'A complicated delivery, your grace, and the appearance of not one but two babies was the explanation. I'm happy to tell you that both mother and babies are doing well. I have yet to put my bag in whatever chamber I've been designated.'

'Then, you must do so. I don't know if you're aware of this, but Mama is unwell. She has taken a strong sleeping draught and won't be awake until the morning but I would like you to visit her before you leave. She seemed quite well to me but was insistent that she felt the mania building inside.'

'I shall speak to her grace tomorrow. I'm sorry that I missed the ceremony and I'm looking forward to attending the ball this evening.'

Richard took her hand and the doctor seemed about to say something but then changed his mind. As they were returning to the festivities she asked about the man who'd tried to force himself upon her sister.

'What are you intending to do with him? You can hardly leave him where he is. If he dies then all three of you could be labelled murderers.'

'We can't risk him speaking to anyone. Surely, you don't want word of Beth's behaviour to become a topic of conversation?'

She pulled her hand away. 'As you so often say to me, my dear, I don't give a damn what anybody says. Our family is a law unto itself and we can do as we please. I won't have that man's death

59

on my conscience. For all we know he thought Beth a willing partner and had no idea of her identity or impairment.'

'God's teeth! That hadn't occurred to me.' He spun on the spot and yelled back up the stairs. He might no longer be a soldier but his voice was loud enough to be heard several miles away. 'Patrick, at the double, man. We've work to do before we can go out and enjoy ourselves.'

Patrick arrived so speedily he almost fell head first when he stopped. Richard explained and both the doctor and Miss Westley overheard.

'We'll move him together, your grace, and find him somewhere more comfortable. Your staff are loyal and won't talk of this, I'm sure.'

'We can do the same as we did with you, Patrick, when you were knocked senseless by the soldiers trying to take you back as a deserter. We shall oust another unfortunate servant from his room and put this person in his bed.'

Miss Westley looked relieved rather than dismayed at the conversation. 'Your grace, I'm more familiar with the workings of the servants' quarters. Please allow me to make the necessary arrangements.'

Eventually, the stranger was more comfortable in an upper servant's room and the five of them were able to stroll out to join the merrymakers and enjoy an ascent in the air balloon.

4

Hannah enjoyed watching Patrick throwing a wooden ball at a row of flowerpots
in order to win her admiration. He was
deadly accurate and demolished all of
them much to the annoyance of the stall-
holder and the amusement of the other
spectators.

'What next, Hannah? Do you think it's
time to head towards the balloon? Will
the duke and duchess have finished with
their business in the Romany camp?'

She loved hearing him speak her name.
They had dispensed with formality and
also with the company of the doctor who
at some point had absented himself. She
was ashamed to admit that she'd not
noticed him go.

'Let's go to the balloon. I've still not
quite decided if I wish to accompany
you but I'll make my decision when I get
there.' The balloon was at that moment
anchored to the ground awaiting the

next occupants. It really was an impressive sight, as big as a house but much prettier.

When they approached the long queue of eager aeronauts she squeezed his arm. 'It hardly seems fair to take someone else's place. We should really join the end of the line, Patrick.'

'Our companions are waving to us from the front so you have no choice, my dear. Here, allow me to put your cloak around your shoulders so you're ready to clamber in.'

She was handed into the basket before she had time to consider refusing. It was commodious basket and able to take four passengers as well as the pilot. When Patrick put his arm around her she didn't object. Then with a shudder the balloon began a stately ascent. It became colder almost immediately and she was glad she had the protection of her cloak.

'My word, how different the world looks from up here. We can see for miles — look, Richard, there's Denchester and the Dower House.'

The duke leaned perilously over the edge and made the basket rock alarmingly. The pilot asked him to desist and he did so with an apologetic smile. They were on one side and she and Patrick were peering over the other. She was relieved that the sides of the basket came up to her shoulders which made her feel a trifle safer.

'People look like toys down there, Patrick, and it's so much quieter up here. I do believe that I would agree to a proper flight if one was available sometime.'

The pilot overheard this comment. 'That can easily be arranged, miss, but the only safe time to fly is at dawn and then only if the weather's clement.'

'How interesting, perhaps another day this can be arranged.'

The ascent was over too soon and the four men on the winches below soon wound them down. Lady Sarah and Paul were waiting to greet them.

'We went up a while ago, which was most invigorating. Did you enjoy it?' Paul asked.

'So much so, that I'm tempted to do it again but that wouldn't be fair on the others waiting,' she said with a smile.

'Your grace, I know I've been given the afternoon free but I'm not comfortable enjoying myself knowing that Beth has yet to be bathed and changed and tell us her side of the story.'

'I was about to say the same thing, Miss Westley. Shall we leave the gentlemen and make our way to the house? Anyway, it will soon be time to begin our preparations for the ball.'

Hannah noticed there was a steady exodus of smartly dressed ladies and gentlemen from the grounds as they headed towards their carriages which had been summoned. No one, apart from the doctor, was staying in the house so everybody was obliged to go home and change into their finery for the evening's event.

There was no sign of any of the villagers departing as their evening entertainment didn't require a change of raiment. There were two hogs roasting over spits at this very moment and there were dozens of barrels of ale being tapped and made ready in the marquee that had been the venue for the grand wedding breakfast earlier.

Beth was not only awake, she was in a fresh gown, her hair neatly braided, and was happily eating nursery tea with Paul's mother. There were two chambermaids in attendance.

'Miss Westley, I'm having scones with cream and conserve for my tea. Would you like one?'

'No, thank you, sweetheart. Are you feeling better after your sleep?'

'Aunt Paula has been here with me and helped me to bathe and change. I don't like being dirty.'

'That was very kind of her. Shall I sit with you and tell you about my trip in the balloon so Mrs Marchand can snatch a few minutes to herself?'

'Yes, yes, I want to hear everything you did. Aunt Paula says that maybe the balloon will come back another time and I can have my ride in it after all.'

'I think that's an excellent notion. I,

too, wish to enjoy for a second time the delights of seeing the world from the point of view of a bird.' She waved away the maids and they disappeared through the servants' door.

When they were alone she thought it the right time to mention the unpleasant interlude. 'Beth, my dear, can you tell me how you came to be with that gentleman? I don't believe you'd been introduced.'

'I was playing with the dogs, I think they remembered me from when I was there a few weeks ago, and Jeremy came over and was throwing sticks for them.'

'Did he tell you his full name? I don't think I've met anyone called Jeremy.'

'He did, he told me he was Mr Jeremy Carstairs. I misremember where he said he lived, but it's not somewhere I'd heard of.'

'Did you tell him who you were?'

'I told him I was Beth and that I lived close by. The dogs went away and I was sad so he said we could sit together somewhere privately and he would tell me a story to keep me entertained.'

'So, that explains why you had grass stains your gown. You should know better than to sit on the grass without a rug being put down first. Did he tell you an interesting story? Could you tell me what it was?'

Beth frowned. 'He didn't tell me anything. He wanted to kiss me and I didn't like it. Then the dogs came back and growled at him. We jumped up and we laughed and ran away but then Mr O'Riley arrived and knocked him over. I think that was very unkind of him, don't you?'

'I think it was the right thing to do. Mr Carstairs was behaving very badly. You should know better than to talk to anyone you haven't been properly introduced to.' She poured herself a glass of lemonade and drank it as if it was the most delicious thing in the world. When she was certain Beth wasn't going to become upset she continued her gentle questioning.

'I do hope nobody saw you misbehave,

my dear, it would be most upsetting if people were to talk about it on your sister's wedding day.'

'Nobody saw me. I ran down the path that Mr O'Riley brought me home by. I don't think anyone even knew I was there.'

'I can hear Mrs Marchand about to come in. I have to change for the ball, but I'll come in and show you my lovely new gown before I go down.'

Hannah was sure that this Mr Carstairs had intended to force his attentions on Beth, that he deserved whatever punishment his grace thought appropriate, and thanked the good Lord that nothing untoward had taken place.

★ ★ ★

Patrick knew it would be an hour or more before the gig could be fetched around for him as so many of the guests were before him in their desire to depart. He could walk the distance more quickly. He spoke to the head groom and

69

arranged for the carriage to be sent to the Dower House as soon as possible.

There was a bath waiting for him — a luxury he enjoyed but, if he was honest, thought unnecessary. A good wash under the yard pump had been enough for him for years and he thought sitting in a hip bath with his feet over the end a silly way to get clean.

His valet had his evening rig ready for him and he was waiting for the gig when it trundled up. The sound of the revelry, continuing in the grounds unabated, this time made him smile. Hannah had found him before he left and repeated everything that Beth had told her. He'd asked her not to share the information but leave him to inform his grace. She had been only too happy to pass the responsibility onto him.

There'd been no opportunity to speak to the duke and the thought of what might be decided when he heard cast a shadow over his happiness at the thought of spending a few hours next to the young woman he loved. He'd never thought to be struck by this particular affliction, thought himself too old and too tough to be involved in such nonsense. Then his grace had fallen neck over crop for his duchess and then Paul, even more speedily, had given his heart to Lady Sarah. Like a head cold — love must be catching.

When he'd been serving under Major Richard Sinclair, as he'd been known then, any soldier unwise enough to rape a girl, or even attempt to do so, would be strung up in short order. The men knew justice would be swift and brutal and thankfully there had only been one enlisted man executed for this crime in all the years he and the major had been together.

Now his blood had cooled, his fury lessened, he no longer thought the culprit should be executed. The villain had a broken jaw — he would try and persuade his employer that this was sufficient punishment. That said, if he was asked to do what he'd offered he wouldn't hesitate. He was loyal to the duke to his core.

He'd deliberately planned his arrival ahead of the other guests as he was to dine with the family before the ball began. He checked his battered, silver pocket watch. Dinner was served at six o'clock — not country hours here — which gave him an hour to find his grace and have this difficult conversation. It was unlikely that his quarry would already be upstairs as he didn't take kindly to all the fuss that being a member of the aristocracy meant he was forced to conform with.

'Patrick, just the man I wanted to speak to. I see you're ready for the fray. Amanda's getting dressed. It doesn't take me an hour to change my raiment. Good God — remember the days when we were roused from our cots and leading our men into battle in less than half an hour?'

They strolled onto the terrace where things were quieter now as those with young children had already departed, the balloon remained inflated but firmly tethered, the various performers had gone, but several dozen were already making merry in the marquee.

They leaned their backs against the sun-warmed wall and stood in companionable silence for a few moments. 'Your grace, Hannah had the full story from Lady Beth.' He quickly regaled him with the unpalatable truth.

'I have information for you on this matter. Carstairs, it appears, is the eldest son of the vicar — he's just been sent down from Oxford in disgrace. I never met this rogue, but have continued to meet the expense of his education as my predecessor did.'

It was as if a large stone had settled in his chest. 'Then he knew exactly who she was and what he was attempting to do. Bugger me! Do you think the little turd thought to persuade you to let him marry her or was he going to resort to blackmail?'

'His father conducted my wedding ceremony and today has married Sarah and Paul. If he'd been anyone else I'd not have thought twice about disposing of him but in all conscience I can't now deal out the justice he deserves. What am I to do, Patrick?'

'I can't fathom why we didn't recognise the name.'

'Exactly so. It just didn't occur to me that he could have any connection to the vicar who is a respectable and intelligent man. How did he come to have such a renegade for a son?'

'Another thing, why had he got frayed cuffs and worn boots? His pa's a well-turned-out sort of gentleman.'

'The only sensible explanation to this conundrum is that the vicar isn't aware that his son is in the vicinity. My valet obtained this information from one of the villagers without revealing the reason for his question.'

'There's nothing we can do about it tonight, sir, Carstairs is in a locked room and there's someone keeping an eye on him. According to the quack the laudanum he administered for the pain will keep him comatose until the morning. No need to do anything hasty.'

'I don't like to keep Amanda in the

dark but this is one thing I'm not going to share with her. It's better if the ladies don't know the identity of the bastard. Excuse me, my friend, I must change. Those guests who are returning to dine with us before the ball will be arriving shortly.'

★ ★ ★

Patrick was delighted to find himself seated next to Hannah and Peterson didn't appear bothered that he was at the far end of the table. Maybe he'd mistaken the matter and the doctor wasn't interested. During the evening he occasionally glanced in Peterson's direction and at no time did he see him looking at her.

Whatever had been served, there had been half a dozen removes with each course, was delicious but he much preferred plain fare. If there must be three courses then why was there this rigmarole of having several different plates to choose from. None of which, in his opinion, complemented each other.

'Patrick, why are you scowling at that blanc-mange? Does the colour offend you?' Hannah tapped his hand with her spoon.

'I'd rather have a figgy pudding, my dear, than this fancy dessert.'

'Blanc-mange is hardly the height of elegance or at all elaborate. There's some sort of fruit tart further down the table, why don't you have that instead?'

She beckoned to a hovering footman and he fetched the pie and then cut him a generous slice. There was thick, fresh cream to pour over it. 'Thank you, this is quite delicious. However, I'm glad the footmen took that wobbling monstrosity away.'

Eventually, the duchess rose and the ladies followed, all the gentlemen also stood whilst they trooped out leaving them to circulate the port. Under normal circumstances his grace would have cut this short, he preferred to spend his time with his wife, but tonight was different.

Apart from himself, the duke, and Paul there were also seven other gentlemen who were the most prestigious in the area. There were two baronets, two lords, an earl and two very wealthy and titled landowners.

* * *

Amanda understood immediately why Richard didn't appear to join them in the drawing room within the usual fifteen minutes. Now was the perfect opportunity for him to elicit any information that might be circulating about the unpleasant incident.

The ladies chatted about the wedding, the novelty of eating wedding breakfast in a tent, and the excitement of ascending in a balloon. Amanda sat with Sarah and indicated that Hannah — she was no longer to be called by her full name after this afternoon — join her at a small group of chairs away from the others.

Obviously they couldn't discuss Beth so she turned the conversation to what might be expected to happen both inside and outside during the remainder of the evening.

'I've had the most perfect day, Amanda, and being able to dance as many times as I want to with Paul tonight will be the perfect ending. He suddenly insists that we leave at first light and my trunks are already downstairs waiting to be put in the carriage in which our personal attendants will travel.'

'It will take you several days to get to the Lake District, my love, so better to set off early. I gather that he's reserved rooms for you at the very best inns. The journey will be taken slowly and will be as much part of your honeymoon as the weeks you intend to reside in that lovely area.

'The only drawback is that, Sarah, you won't be able to speak to Mama before you leave.'

'I spent time with her yesterday. She was very subdued and anxious but I saw no sign of the violence and confusion that happened last time. I do hope she

78

isn't avoiding my wedding because she disapproves of my choice.'

'She is as delighted as I am, and everyone else is. It is a small concern that you've known him such a short time but even a blind man could see you are perfectly suited and completely in love with each other.'

Hannah kept glancing at the double doors that led to the formal dining room and she thought she guessed the reason. 'Hannah, do you and Patrick have an understanding?'

'No, that is, I don't know. I know that Doctor Peterson might be considered a better choice but somehow I find myself drawn to Patrick.'

'You've known him for over a year, he's been a good friend to you and to all of us. You must go where your heart leads you. He's part of the family already in a way that I don't believe Doctor Peterson ever could be. Richard and he have been firm friends for a decade and that should be recommendation enough for any lady.'

Hannah nodded and her eyes shone. She'd never looked lovelier. Small wonder that two eligible gentlemen were eager to gain her hand.

'Do I have your blessing? I would continue to take care of Beth, have no concerns on that score.'

'I know Richard would be delighted. I promise I'll say nothing to him until things are settled between you.'

5

Hannah wondered if she was being a little premature in discussing a possible match between her and Patrick. After all, hadn't he had a year to suggest such a thing but until today had not shown her any special attention. She smiled at her silliness. Of course he hadn't said anything as he still didn't know if he was going to be arrested as a deserter and forced to re-enlist for five years. Until that was settled he would feel honour-bound not to tie her to him.

The doors opened at last and he was standing behind the duke, his startling red hair and his impressive size made him easy to see as he was taller even than his grace. He looked across the drawing room and his smile made her warm all over.

He said something to the duke as he passed and then strode across to join her. 'The other guests are beginning to arrive, Hannah, so we've no time to talk privately.'

'I'm content to be in your company, Patrick, and intend to enjoy every minute of this occasion. I've only ever attended one other such event and was never a genuine guest before.'

'Although we might be considered somewhat older than the other young sprigs and their partners, I believe I can safely say that we make a handsome couple.' He picked up a fold in the skirt of her gown and let the silk slip through his fingers. 'Is this colour peach or called something more exciting? You look quite beautiful tonight — I'll be the envy of every gentleman here.'

'I come a poor third to her grace and Lady Sarah, but thank you for your compliment. However, I'm not sure mentioning my maturity was tactful. Some might consider that at the age of four and twenty I am at my last prayers.'

'I didn't know exactly how old you are, thank you for telling me. I'm nine and twenty — in my prime — but then gentlemen consider themselves in their prime until they are in their fifties.'

'Are you fishing for compliments, sir? You are a handsome man but if I'm being brutally honest, I prefer you in your everyday clothes. Black doesn't suit your colouring.'

He laughed as she'd hoped he would. 'I always thought I cut a fine figure in my best regimentals. I still have them — would you like to see me dressed in my uniform?'

She detected there was more to this light-hearted question and all desire to laugh disappeared. 'I hope you don't have to wear those again, Patrick, but if you do, it won't change the way I feel about you.' She hadn't intended to blurt out something so revealing but now he knew how she felt.

His eyes blazed. 'Will you walk with me on the terrace until the music starts, Hannah?'

She looped her hand through his arm and could feel the tension in the muscles beneath her fingers. There were two other couples enjoying the early evening sunshine and watching the antics of the less fortunate who had obviously, from their lively behaviour, already broached the barrels of ale intended for the evening party.

They walked to the far end, away from prying eyes, and then he turned. He took both her hands in his. 'I love you, Hannah, and can hardly believe my luck that you reciprocate my feelings. You understand my perilous situation and must know that I cannot make you an offer until matters are settled.'

'I think I would make an excellent soldier's wife, Patrick, and I'm quite prepared to follow the drum. I never thought to marry and can hardly credit that I have two gentlemen interested in me.' His expression changed and she wished she hadn't been quite so honest. 'Doctor Peterson hasn't spoken in so many words, but I know that if I gave him the slightest hint that I was interested he would make me an offer. He's too much of a gentleman to do anything that might embarrass me.'

'You would do better to marry him, he can give you so much more than I. I'm not much more than a rough soldier and he's an educated gentleman. I'll never own my own property, I'll always be dependent on the good offices of the duke. I've no idea where we would live as once the new house is completed the dowager duchess and her entourage will wish to live in the Dower House.'

'We've both waited many years to find each other, there's no rush to make this official. Just knowing that you return my feelings, that one day we can be together, God willing, will be enough for me at present.'

He twisted so his bulk was between her and anyone wandering about on the terrace. Then he cupped her face and kissed her. The touch of his lips confirmed what she already knew. She would marry Patrick or remain a spinster.

'We could marry immediately, my love, make it three weddings in a row. Then, whatever happens, we'll have a few weeks together. If you go away to fight you might well be killed.'

He drew her closer so her cheek was resting against his chest. 'It's a grand thought, sweetheart, but I could leave you carrying my child . . . '

'That would make losing you a little more bearable. I would always be part of this family and so would a child. Why should we deny ourselves what little time we might have?'

'Let me think on it. You're a beautiful young woman and if I wasn't here then you could marry Peterson.'

She stood on tiptoe and was the one to initiate a kiss. This time was quite different, she was swept along by a feeling so intense that, if he hadn't been holding her, she might have collapsed in a puddle of silk at his feet.

Eventually he raised his head. She was breathless but thought she'd proved her point. 'If I can't marry you, Patrick, I'll not marry anyone. I think it highly unlikely the doctor would want to make me his wife when he would always be second best.'

There was a constant rattle of carriages arriving which meant the ball would be beginning soon. Belatedly she realised that although the two couples on the terrace with them had seen nothing, anyone in the gardens — and there were dozens of them — would have witnessed she and Patrick behaving disgracefully.

'What's wrong?' He was aware immediately that she was upset.

'We should have been more circumspect, my dear, everything we did was in full view to those enjoying the garden party down there.'

He said something extremely impolite and she raised her eyebrows. He grinned but didn't apologise. 'We should have known better especially after what happened with Beth this morning.' He held out his hand and she placed hers within it. 'Too late for regrets, my angel, I'll not have anyone tarnish your reputation. Do you wish me to go down on one knee?'

'Absolutely not. We've made sufficient spectacle of ourselves already.' Then she reconsidered. 'Actually, it might be exactly the right thing to do. Then anyone who witnessed our embrace will applaud our actions and not speak ill of us.'

He kept hold of her hand but dropped smoothly to one knee. 'Miss Westley, would you do me the honour of becoming my wife? Please make me the happiest of men.'

'Thank you for your kind offer, Mr O'Riley, I'm delighted to accept.'

He stood up and kissed her again for good measure just in case anyone was in doubt about his intentions.

When he stepped away there was a cheer, albeit a somewhat drunken one, from the gawping crowd. Patrick put his arm around her waist and they turned and waved and received another cheer. Satisfied they'd prevented any unpleasant gossip they hurried inside.

'We must speak to our employers immediately. There must be something in the air as this will be the third engagement in a short space of time that has taken place here.'

★ ★ ★

Patrick kept a tight hold of his precious girl. Speaking to any member of the family was impossible as they were waiting in line to greet their guests.

'It might be some time before they're free. Shall we join the line of guests and pretend that we've just arrived in a carriage? That way we can guarantee they hear our good news before anyone else tells them.'

'It's not an entire fabrication, Patrick, as you did indeed arrive in a carriage a short time ago. I think it's a sensible suggestion although somewhat unusual.'

When they stood in front of the duke and his duchess there was no need to explain why they were there.

'Congratulations, my good friend, I couldn't be happier for both of you. I'll announce your engagement later this evening if you wish me to.'

'No, I thank you, your grace, but this is Paul and Lady Sarah's celebration. Word will spread soon enough as we were seen kissing on the terrace.'

Hannah was being embraced by the duchess and then he too was hugged and Hannah received the same from the duke. Nobody could have been in any doubt that the two of them were intimates of this illustrious family.

He danced four times with his betrothed including a waltz at the end of the evening. Paul had sought him out and added his best wishes to those they'd received from everyone else present.

'I always thought you had feelings for her, but until tonight I wasn't sure that she reciprocated.'

'Neither was I — I'm not certain I should have asked her when things are so undecided. I just pray that word from Horse Guards arrives soon confirming that I'm no longer considered a deserter.'

'Robinson is a good man, he'll have got that letter to the right person by now. He might be an ensign but he's an excellent officer and will go far in the army.'

'Let's hope that you're right. I gather that you and your new bride will be leaving at dawn on your wedding trip. When can we expect you to return?'

'Before the bad weather sets in — so no later than October. I hope you don't intend to tie the knot before then as I'd like to stand up for you if you wish me to.'

'I'd be honoured. I truly hope that I'm still here and not back in regimentals in Portugal. Hannah wants me to marry her immediately just in case that happens but I've no intention of doing so. I'm hoping that if I was forced to go that the quack will step in and take my place and give her a better life than I could.'

'Good luck with that, my friend. I think our women are reluctant to do what's expected of them. If I was you I would marry her immediately and thank God for the opportunity, even if that means Sarah and I won't be there to witness the ceremony.'

They parted with a handshake and Patrick watched him stride away to join his beautiful wife. Lady Sarah looked nothing like her older sister — she had golden curls and blue eyes like Beth. What he found quite extraordinary was the fact that the duke and duchess could be siblings so similar were they in appearance. They were only very distant cousins which was what made their resemblance so odd.

The guests departed, the noise from the revellers outside abated, the ladies retired, leaving the duke and himself to decide on what they would do with the vicar's son.

'Let's repair to my study, Patrick. I've sent for coffee and sandwiches. I fear it's going to be a long night.'

'I heard a while ago that Carstairs is sleeping comfortably and showing no signs of waking.'

It would have been more pleasant outside but voices carried at night and they had no wish to be overheard. It had already been agreed that he would stay the night so he hadn't the prospect of walking four miles in the dark when this conversation was done.

A large silver coffee jug was waiting for

them and alongside was a pile of sandwiches that would have fed half a dozen
hungry soldiers. His host handed him
a glass filled to the brim with cognac.
Once they were settled with their drinks
and food the discussion began.

'If the vicar believes his son to still
be at university then he won't be worried about his absence. This gives us a
week to come to some decision. I fear
that whatever he might promise, whatever bribe he might take — if that's the
route I decided to go — he won't keep
his word. Do you agree?'

'I do, your grace . . . '

'For God's sake, cut rope, Patrick. If
you can't bring yourself to call me Richard then call me Major. I refuse to answer
to your grace.'

'Major, I think you're right to be dubi-
ous about this villain's ability to keep
his trap shut. I'm not comfortable with
murdering the vicar's son — in fact I
wouldn't want to murder anybody's son
in cold blood. I have a suggestion. He
could be put aboard a ship sailing for

the colonies, or India — it would be the making of him and when he returned it wouldn't matter one way or the other what he said to anybody.'

'Press-ganged? I don't think we could put him on board a naval ship, but the idea's sound. I own two trading vessels. Somewhere I've got the information about their whereabouts. It would be a stroke of good fortune if one of them was actually in port or on its way here.'

'Better you're not involved with this, Major. I'll arrange things. I just need to transport him to London docks and then bribe some sailors to take him aboard. Once they're at sea it doesn't matter what he says as he'll have to work his passage. He could be away for two years.'

'He can't be moved until he's fit. How long did the doctor say it would be before he can eat normally?'

'Several weeks at least. His jaw will be bound up until then so he won't be able to speak. Obviously, he can't remain under your roof, but he could be transferred to the Dower House. I've plenty of staff and they're all loyal to the core.'

'We'll move him now, whilst he's comatose. There's bound to be someone awake upstairs who can help us.' He drained his glass and poured them both a second. He grinned making him look years younger. 'If there isn't, there soon will be.' He opened the door and yelled for attention down the passageway.

Patrick choked on his coffee. 'God's teeth, Major, you'll have everybody up now.'

'It's like the old days, my friend, I've not had so much fun in weeks.'

★ ★ ★

Amanda dismissed her maid as soon as she was in her nightgown. She slipped on her robe, pushed her feet into indoor slippers and went to see if Beth and her mother were still sleeping. Mrs Marchand, who insisted she should be addressed by her given name, Paula, in future, was reading in the nursery.

'Your grace, Lady Beth is sleeping

95

peacefully. I've had a truckle bed set up in her bedchamber and will sleep there as promised.'

'If I am to call you Paula in future then you must call me Amanda and desist from using titles when addressing any of the family. Is Hannah abed? Did she give you her good news before she retired?'

'I heard her come up a few minutes ago but she's not been in to speak to me as yet . . .'

There was a rustle of skirts and Hannah appeared, also in her nightwear. 'I was just coming to tell you that Patrick and I are now betrothed. How is Beth?'

Amanda left the two of them chatting quietly and headed for the rooms set aside for her mother and her retainers. She was on the gallery when Richard's voice echoed through the house. What was he thinking? He would have everybody up wanting to know why he was yelling.

Hannah appeared at the top of the nursery stairs. 'Was that his grace shouting for attention?'

'It certainly was. I'm going down to investigate but I think it sensible that only one of us appears incorrectly attired. I'll let you know what all the fuss was about when I come back.'

In this house not all the wall sconces were doused at night — some of them were replenished before the butler retired. This meant it was always possible to move about the place without carrying a candlestick.

She could hear her husband laughing in the study and it sounded as if Patrick was with him. Neither of them were entirely sober.

'Good evening, Richard, might I enquire why you thought it necessary to rouse the entire household in that way?'

His smile, as always, rocked her back on her heels. 'There's something I have to tell you, my love, and I apologise in advance for not doing so earlier.'

She listened to his story in silence. 'That man is the son of our vicar? How unfortunate that is.' Richard and Patrick laughed at her quite sensible remark.

She stared at them attempting to look cross but her mouth began to twitch and soon she was joining in the merriment.

'Have either of you sent word for a closed carriage to be brought round?'

'I'm waiting for someone to come here so I can send them to wake the stables.' He poured himself another generous measure of brandy and Patrick held out his glass for the same. This was quite ridiculous. They were behaving in a most reprehensible manner and this would end in disaster if she didn't intervene.

'Enough brandy, sirs. You need your wits about you and at the moment they have flown. If this is supposed to be a clandestine operation why did you consider it sensible to wake up everybody in the house first and then do the same for the outside men?'

'A good point, my love, well made, don't you think, Patrick? Perhaps it would have been wiser to do this ourselves.'

'Right, Major, I'll fetch Carstairs

whilst you sort out the transport.'

'First I must reassure those I can hear coming to your aid that it was merely drunken high spirits that caused you to shout. I'll send them to bed.' She didn't wait for his response but moved swiftly outside and waylaid the two senior footmen and the butler who were approaching at a run. Satisfied they'd accepted her explanation and were going to their beds she returned to the two inebriated gentlemen.

To her astonishment the room was empty. They hadn't come past her so must have exited via the window. She ran across the room and leaned out. She could hear nothing. Perhaps neither of them had been as drunk as she'd thought. They were soldiers and used to night manoeuvres and would accomplish this transfer without any more interference from herself.

She doused the candles in the study and closed the window. After explaining to Paula and Hannah what the racket had been about she returned to the apartment she shared with Richard. There'd been no need to visit Mama as Hannah had gone in her stead.

She was woken by the slight sound of Richard removing his garments. She pushed herself up onto her elbows and could just see him in the shaft of moonlight that filtered through the shutters. 'Did you accomplish your mission, Major Sinclair?'

'We didn't bother with the carriage, Patrick slung him over a horse and we led him there. He didn't stir and is now secure in the chamber that Beth used to occupy. Patrick's excellent valet has taken over the task of being both guard and nursemaid until Carstairs is fit to become a sailor.'

'I've been thinking, my love, that you need to speak to Mr Carstairs, his father, before you implement your plan. Imagine his distress when he eventually learns that his son is missing.'

'As always, my darling, you have the right of it. However, it will be a *fait accompli* — I don't intend to tell him until his rat of a son is safely on his way.'

'I see. Do you think it might be possible to arrange for him to have sufficient funds given to him to buy his passage back? He would still be absent from the country for a year or more but then we could be sanguine that he would be able to return to his family eventually and . . .'

He slid in beside her and she had no opportunity to finish her sentence. She fell asleep naked in his arms and didn't wake until he leaned over and kissed her. As often happened they both were late for breakfast.

6

Hannah scarcely slept so excited was she at the prospect of becoming Patrick's bride. Whatever his thoughts on the matter she was determined to persuade him one way or another to marry her immediately. Obviously, she couldn't arrange for a special licence but what she could do was visit the vicarage and have the banns called. That would mean in three weeks they could legally marry in the village church. Patrick rarely attended church so was unlikely to hear them being read out at matins.

Although she had been given a further day's leave she had no intention of taking all of it. Beth needed her and Paula must return to her duties as companion to the dowager duchess. Notwithstanding, she was determined to visit the vicarage immediately after breakfast. She tingled all over at the only certain way she could think of to make Patrick change his mind and marry her immediately.

Eventually she fell into so deep sleep she didn't wake until someone came into her room carrying a tray with what smelt like chocolate and sweet morning rolls. This was unheard of — a custom only for the family not for a servant, which was all she was really.

A smiling girl bobbed in a curtsy when she sat up. 'Good morning, miss, I'm Ellie, I'm to be your personal maid. I'm to pack all your belongings and move them down stairs.'

Hannah stared at her unable to comprehend what had been said. 'That can't be correct, Ellie, are you sure you heard aright?'

The tray was placed across her lap and her stomach gurgled in anticipation of this unexpected treat.

'I have that, miss. It comes from her grace herself. You are to be considered as part of the family from now on.'

She could hardly continue to argue with a maid, but as soon as she'd broken her fast she would go and see her grace. Her role was as governess and companion to Beth and as such she had to have her accommodation adjacent to her charge.

'Is Mrs Marchand taking care of Lady Elizabeth?'

The girl looked puzzled at the question. 'No, Nanny and the two nursemaids are doing that. There's Johnny working up here too.'

'Who is Johnny?' The more she heard the less she understood.

'Johnny is a junior footman, and he's to accompany Lady Elizabeth whenever she goes out for a walk. I reckon she'll like having him along as he's a handsome lad.'

This was a highly unsuitable conversation to be having with one's personal maid. 'I intend to ride this morning so please put out my habit. Also, send word to the stables to have a suitable mount ready for me in half an hour.'

* * *

Talking to the duchess must wait until she'd accomplished her own important task. At least she knew she wouldn't bump into Patrick as he had spent the night in his own home back at Denchester. She was a novice rider and was somewhat apprehensive about going out on her own for the first time, but the head groom was well aware of her limitations and would no doubt put her up on the docile mare she'd learned to ride on earlier this summer.

It was no more than two miles to the vicarage and she accomplished this at a steady jog and was feeling far more confident in her abilities by the time she arrived. Dismounting would be a problem and getting back into the saddle even more difficult if there wasn't a mounting block available.

This problem was solved as Mr Carstairs was just leaving as she rode up. 'Good morning, Miss Westley, how can I be of service to you this fine day?'

She handed down to him the paper with the necessary details and he offered his congratulations and promised to do as she asked.

'Do you have a date in mind for the wedding?'

Hannah was finding it more difficult than she'd anticipated to talk to this kind man about her wedding when she knew that his oldest son was about to be shipped off to India for attempting to rape an innocent girl. The fact that the person he'd chosen for his debauchery was the sister of the Duke of Denchester just made the offence so much worse.

'I believe that once the final calling has been made we can marry at the church without giving further notice as long as it is before five of the clock.'

'That is quite correct, Miss Westley. From this I take it that you will be having a simple ceremony, just witnesses, and don't require the church to be decorated in any way.'

'How much notice do we need to give you?'

'None at all, my dear Miss Westley, because if I'm away from home visiting a sick parishioner then my curate can conduct the service in my stead.'

Satisfied she had everything in place now all she had to do was somehow arrange for Patrick to come to her bedchamber or for her to go to his. So absorbed was she in trying to work out how this might be achieved, since she was going to be living on the family floor, that twice the old mare stopped to eat from the hedge.

She trotted back up the drive with the horse still chewing a large mouthful of something tasty that she'd snatched whilst Hannah had been wool-gathering.

So much had changed, and so quickly, that she scarcely knew whether she was on her head or her heels. The grounds were full of eager labourers dismantling the various booths and tents from yesterday's celebrations. It might take some time for the grass to recover its former lushness after being trampled on so thoroughly yesterday.

The aeronauts were packing their balloon onto a large diligence drawn by two farm horses. One day she would ask Patrick to take her on a real flight — but obviously not today. She entered through the side door and was immediately met by a footman who told her that she was expected in the drawing room immediately.

She gathered up the trailing skirt of her habit and hurried down the passageway. What disaster had occurred in her absence? She really should have asked permission before leaving the estate as she had. The church clock had struck as she'd left the vicarage so it could hardly be later than ten o'clock.

'There you are, Hannah, you must have so many questions. Come in and sit down, coffee will be fetched for us immediately. Are you hungry after your ride?' Her grace looked quite radiant and beckoned her over as if she was someone other than a governess.

'I shouldn't be in here until I've changed. I smell of horse . . . '

'Fiddlesticks to that. If I cared about such things then Richard would soon have cured me of it. Please sit down.'

She did as she was told and waited to hear why she'd suddenly been elevated from employee to dear friend or distant relative.

'I should have asked permission before taking the mare, but I had something most urgent to do.'

'Richard and I have decided that you and Patrick are now part of our family. Consider yourselves under his protection, and in future you will only need to ask permission as a daughter or sister would from the head of the household.'

'Am I not to take care of Beth? I was surprised to find her usual retainers back on duty when I thought they had been dismissed.'

'As my sister came to no real harm we reconsidered and they were, quite naturally, overjoyed to be reinstated. You can be very sure that nothing like that will ever happen again. I intend to employ someone else to take over as companion and governess and I'm hoping that you will help me select a suitable candidate.'

This nonsense had gone on long enough. 'Forgive me, but this makes no sense to me. I'm not related to any of you in any way and neither is Patrick. Why should the duke be responsible for my upkeep?'

'I told Richard you would say this, but he is relying on me to persuade you to change your mind. Patrick is his man of affairs, that's true, which makes him an employee of sorts. However, he is first and foremost like a brother to him. They have been side by side through the most terrible battles, are closer than most siblings are because of this.'

'So, I am being included in his generosity because I am betrothed to Patrick?'

'No, I think of you as another sister. You've been part of this family for years — remember you were companion to Sarah and I before our papa died. Everyone residing under this roof is considered a blood relation.' She laughed at the absurdity of her comment. 'Obviously, I'm not including the staff in this statement.'

'Then thank you, I'm delighted and overwhelmed to accept your generosity. Now, forgive me, I'm not comfortable sitting here smelling of the stables. It won't take me long to change. I need to talk to you about something else.' She smiled knowing that Amanda — no, her grace, she wasn't comfortable using her given name — would help her with her shocking plan to seduce Patrick into marrying her in three weeks' time.

* * *

Patrick was up with the lark none the worse for his excessive consumption of brandy the night before. He was fortunate in that he didn't suffer from the after-effects of alcohol like others did. He could drink what he wanted, remain upright and clear-headed when others were under the table, and this had often proved invaluable in his years as a soldier.

He went to check that his unwelcome guest was awake as there were one or two things he wanted to say to him. Carstairs was propped up in bed and his eyes widened when he saw Patrick walk in. Good. He wanted the little bastard to be terrified.

'I know who you are, I know what you did and if you wish to carry on living you will do as you're told and make no attempt to leave this room. Do you understand?'

The young man attempted to nod but it was obviously so painful he couldn't complete the gesture. Patrick felt a moment of sympathy, of regret for having broken his jaw. Then he considered what would have happened to Carstairs if the major had got hold of him first. On balance, a broken jaw was better than a broken neck.

'Good. You will be fed and taken care of whilst it's decided what will become of you. If you'd been in my brigade you would now be hanging from the nearest tree. Think yourself lucky to still be alive — although I can't guarantee how much longer that'll last.'

His valet locked the door and grinned. 'That'll keep the little bugger quiet, sir. I've put your shaving water out and there's been a message from his grace. I put it beside the hot water.'

Patrick was laughing as he returned to his bedchamber. He hadn't intended to shave this morning, thought it a waste of time and energy and was quite happy to remain without recourse to the razor for several days at a stretch. John obviously had other ideas and wished to keep his master looking like the gentleman he obviously wasn't.

He broke the seal on the letter and read it with incredulity. The world had gone mad this past day. The major insisted that he moved back to Radley Manor and considered himself as a member of the family not an employee. He was expected to join the family for luncheon.

He looked around with amusement as he saw that his trunks were half-packed already. The letter hadn't been opened so obviously the groom who'd delivered it had somehow learned the contents. It was all very well for Richard — he might as well give in and use his given name if he was to be considered a relative in future — to tell him to appear by midday but it would take him several hours to pack the ledgers and papers that he needed from the study. As he was to do Paul's work as the estate manager alongside his own for the next few weeks this meant that these ledgers and documents must also be packed.

God knows where he and Paul would be expected to work at the Manor — one thing was quite certain he didn't intend to be a drain on anyone's pocket. He would earn his keep as he'd always done. Moving also meant he would be obliged to leave behind his excellent valet and he'd become used to his efficient services.

The baggage cart arrived and the four grooms who'd come with it shifted his trunks — Paul's belongings had already been moved — and then carried out the boxes of papers. The staff at the Dower House was being reduced as there would only be Carstairs and his carer living there now. One groom remained to take care of the two horses left behind.

He rode his own beast, a groom drove the cart, and the other two rode the spare horses. Things were moving too fast for him. He liked time to contemplate decisions and wasn't comfortable with being rushed. He had always been the voice of reason in times of danger when Richard had wanted to do something rash.

Living under the same roof as Hannah and not being able to share her bed was going to be difficult. He'd had women, too many to count, during his life but had never been in love. The brief liaisons he'd indulged in had been with light-skirts and camp followers. He'd always taken care of them when they parted and was convinced that he'd left behind no unwanted babies.

This probably meant he was incapable of fathering a child but only time would tell. His mouth curved. He was going to have a damn good try — that was for sure.

When he entered the house the butler was waiting to inform him that Richard was in his study. Patrick strolled along the wide passageway looking at things differently now this was to be his permanent home. Then, as he was about to knock on the door, he froze. He couldn't marry Hannah unless he had somewhere for them to live and he could hardly set up home here. Radley Manor was a spacious house but once the inevitable babies started to arrive it would soon become overcrowded.

'Don't dawdle out there, Patrick, there are things we need to discuss before we can breakfast.' Richard had somehow worked out he was outside the door.

'Good morning, at least I thought it was until I realised that being obliged to move here means I can't now marry Hannah as I've nowhere of my own to take her.'

'Sit down, man, and let me explain.' Richard waited until he was seated before continuing. 'This house is big enough for a dozen families. My mother-in-law has her own rooms, Sarah and Paul have the east wing, Amanda and I occupy the central section of this house and when you marry Hannah you can live in the west wing.'

'I would like to have been consulted, Richard, I don't take kindly to being manipulated. Why in God's good name do you wish to have us all under this roof?'

'Do you want my honest answer?'

'I do, of course I do. What's going on that I don't know about?'

'If you and Paul are here then I can take Amanda on an extended wedding trip. Things have changed between us recently and I want to spend time alone with her and discover why she's no longer as happy as she was.'

'I can tell you one reason. For three years she ran the estates, managed on a pittance compared to the income she was used to before. Since you turned up she's nothing much to do.'

'That's my interpretation of the situation too. Being a lady of leisure doesn't suit my wife any more than it suits me to be idle. If you and Paul can run things for me then I intend to be away for a year. I'll stay in contact and you and Paul can make decisions in my name.'

'And the new house?'

'I'm certain between the two of you you can deal with any problems that might arise. Sarah knows exactly what Amanda would like in the way of furniture, colour and so on. The new house isn't as vast as the original but has more than forty chambers. Paul and Sarah will remain here but I'm hoping that you and Hannah will make your permanent home with us. I'll make over an entire wing to you so you can be independent.'

'And what if they return to arrest me in your absence?'

'I don't intend to leave until Carstairs has been dispatched on his journey and your status as a civilian has been agreed.'

'Forgive me for saying so, old friend, but I can see one flaw in your plans. You can hardly gallivant about the world if Amanda's in an interesting condition.'

'Being pregnant isn't an illness, Patrick, it's as natural for a woman to have a child as it is for a man to fight.' Richard smiled at his comparison.

'Not every woman has an easy time. It won't matter if I don't have children, although I'd like a nursery full, but you must have an heir. Maybe it would be sensible to wait until one arrives before you set off on your travels.'

Richard looked at him as if he was an escapee from an asylum. 'Do you honestly think that Amanda would agree to leave a child behind whilst we went off for months? No — if we're going to travel, which I promised her we would — we must do it now before our first child arrives.'

7

Amanda was delighted to have both Patrick and Hannah included in the family as she'd been dreading Sarah going away for months. Mama, after a long conversation with the doctor, decided that she'd been a little premature in locking herself away and she too was going to join them for dinner in future.

It took a further day for the grounds to be restored to their usual immaculate condition. The highlight of the day, apart from her sister's wedding, had been the ascent in the balloon and Richard had promised to get the aeronauts to come back in the autumn when Sarah and Paul were home from their trip.

Hannah had settled into her new position and Beth, although somewhat more subdued than usual, showed no ill effects from her unpleasant experience. Dining was now something to be looked forward to and gave the ladies an opportunity to change into something elegant.

A week after the wedding she was in her habit and ready to go out for a hack with Hannah who was becoming a competent horsewoman. Today they rode to a pretty wood about two miles from home but still within the boundaries of Radley Manor.

'Shall we dismount here? We can let the horses graze and we can sit in the shade and enjoy the view.'

'I was going to suggest that we did exactly that, as there's something I need to discuss with you most urgently.'

She was intrigued. It had to be something to do with Patrick and there was nothing she liked more than being involved in someone else's affairs.

'Tell me, is something amiss between the two of you?'

'Exactly the opposite. We've never been happier and the more time we spend together the more we find we have in common despite the disparity of our backgrounds.' She hesitated and her cheeks flushed.

'Are you concerned about what happens in the marriage bed?'

'Not exactly, but it is on that subject that I wish to get your opinion and advice.'

When Hannah had finished explaining her reasons for wishing to entice Patrick into her bed without the benefit of clergy she was entirely behind the disgraceful scheme.

'I'm surprised word hasn't reached us that the banns have been called once already. I think it wise if you wait to put your plan into motion until you can legally tie the knot. Unfortunately, Patrick can drink quantities of alcohol without showing ill effects.'

'I only have to have two glasses of champagne, or any wine, and become quite giddy.'

'Then that's what you must do. I'll make sure that champagne is served that night and you can pretend to be in your cups. Patrick, being a gallant gentleman, will offer to carry you to your bedchamber. Make sure that your maid has the evening off.'

'I'm not sure that will work. As you've just pointed out quite rightly, Patrick's a gentleman and wouldn't take advantage of such a situation.'

'Once you have him to yourself I'm sure you can convince him that it's you that's taking advantage of him. I doubt that any gentleman who loves his lady as much as he loves you will be able to resist such temptation.'

'Then perhaps we could hold an informal supper party and invite some neighbours next month?'

'I'm not sure that would be a good idea as someone would be bound to mention that they'd heard your names mentioned at matins. Unless you're prepared to confess to Patrick what you plan, I think it best if we don't have anyone but family here for the moment.'

'I've always considered myself a sensible person but since I fell in love with him I'm acting like a giddy schoolgirl. Being in love is very unsettling.'

Neither of them brought up the subject of Patrick being considered a deserter because he didn't report back for duty last year even though he'd only got a few weeks of his five years to complete. Richard seemed sanguine that there'd be no further Provost marshals turning up to arrest him.

'By the by, there's a candidate for your former position arriving tomorrow. Miss Parsons comes highly recommended and has had experience with a girl who has Beth's disability.'

'I find it quite remarkable that someone as volatile as her has accepted the change in her circumstances so readily. Spending just a few hours every day with her seems to have improved our relationship. I hope I can continue to do so when the new person arrives.'

'You are as a sister to her now and can spend as much or as little time in her company as you wish. I know it will take a little time to adjust, but for Richard and I this new arrangement is ideal. There's nothing he likes better than sitting reminiscing with his friend about his former life.' She sighed. 'I fear he misses the excitement, the comraderie, and finds married life dull by comparison.'

'He was reluctant to take on his title and the responsibilities that came with it, I recall. It was falling in love with you that changed his mind.'

'Oh, do you think so? There's been so much excitement in the past year, I can't understand why I feel so low in spirits at the moment.'

'When you leave for your adventure in a few weeks you'll feel more the thing. I envy you the opportunity to travel all over the world.'

'Adventure? I know nothing about this.' She jumped up her heart pounding. 'I wondered why he's been so secretive, sending people off with letters to heaven knows where. We must return at once so I can find out exactly what he's planned.'

'Oh dear, I'd no idea you didn't know. Patrick didn't tell me it was being kept a secret from you.'

'I'm glad you did let the information slip. There's nothing I like better than planning — sometimes I think the actuality less exciting than what comes before. I refuse to be excluded from this trip a moment longer.'

★ ★ ★

Hannah needed assistance to regain the saddle whereas her companion was able to mount without help by letting down the stirrup iron. They cantered most of the way back and she was somewhat relieved to arrive at the stable yard without having parted company with her docile mare.

'I really shouldn't have said anything. I think both Patrick and the duke are going to be cross with me.'

'Fiddlesticks to that! I'm delighted that you told me so what the gentlemen think is irrelevant.'

Hannah decided to invite Beth to go for a walk around the lake before luncheon. This would mean she would be able to keep her distance from those that would no doubt be wishing to give her a bear-garden jaw.

After spending a pleasant hour or so with her former charge she was ready to brave the possible consequences of her blurting out the secret. In her favour was the fact that she'd no idea it was a secret, but she doubted that would help smooth things over.

Patrick and his grace were arguing in the entrance hall and their voices echoed up the passageway. Something was amiss. She was about to run towards the staircase but then realised it was none of her business. She stopped but could hear quite clearly what they were saying and so would anyone else in the house.

'God dammit to hell, Patrick. I thought this matter settled. They are damn fools at Horse Guards. Don't do anything precipitate but wait until we hear from Wellington. My letters must have reached him and the reply be on its way.'

'I've no choice. Either I re-enlist or I'm hung as a deserter. There's no middle ground offered. I don't intend to tell Hannah, better to spend our last evening happy. I'll write her a letter which you must give her after I've gone.'

'You have until tomorrow before you need to depart for London. At least this time they aren't sending anyone to arrest you, but treating you as a gentleman.'

'Small comfort, Richard. I've already made my decision. I won't go to the idiots who wrote this letter but travel directly to Spain and hand myself in to Wellington. Hopefully, he'll listen to reason, remember how well we served him in India, and let me go.'

She didn't wait to hear any more but slowly backed away biting her lip to stop the tears. They didn't have three weeks — they didn't have any time at all. Patrick had made his decision without consulting her and she'd done the same.

Somehow she would pretend she didn't know his dreadful news, say good night as always. But, once the house was quiet she would make her way to his bedchamber and force the issue. If her friend was correct, then if she presented herself naked in his bed he wouldn't be able to resist.

She might never see him again and she'd no wish to die a maiden. If sharing her body with him gave her his child then that would be a bonus. If it meant she had to retire to a small cottage somewhere in the duke's demesne, then so be it. Doing this would also mean that, whatever the temptation, she'd never accept an offer from a man she didn't love. No gentleman would want used goods.

Did she have the courage to join them in the drawing room and act as if her heart wasn't breaking? She put her shoulders back, straightened her spine, and walked briskly to the staircase. Every moment she could spend with her beloved Patrick, however difficult it might be for her, wasn't to be missed.

The only positive she could take from this disaster was the fact that her indiscretion would no longer seem important to the gentlemen. The drawing room was empty but the doors that led onto the terrace were standing open and she could hear them talking outside.

His grace was standing shoulder to shoulder with Patrick facing the garden and her grace was sitting on her own on one of the marble seats. Her friend looked as miserable as she felt. Something was wrong and she feared it was her fault.

'Hannah, I was about to send out a search party. I saw you return from your walk with my sister half an hour ago.'

'To be honest, I was somewhat worried about joining you after telling you something you weren't supposed to know.'

'I confronted him about this exciting foreign trip and he told me my information was incorrect. He has no plans to take me anywhere at present.'

'How disappointing for you. Did you ask him why he'd changed his mind?'

'I can't tell you how upset I am at his behaviour. He brushed me off as if I was of no account, as if he had other things of more importance to consider. I'll tell you verbatim what he said to me. "I did talk of such a scheme with Patrick, but never seriously considered leaving England. You shouldn't listen to gossip." I wanted to punch him but turned my back on him instead.'

Hannah knew why he was distracted but this was a secret she intended to keep. Once Patrick had gone then her grace would know the reason why her husband was angry and upset. Hopefully, both of them would be so preoccupied by the departure, they would never hear about her tryst with her betrothed. She could remain in her apartment with her grief confident that they wouldn't intrude until they thought her ready to rejoin them.

'It's not like your husband to be so dismissive. There must be something grave afoot to make our gentlemen so stern. I expect we'll hear about it eventually but until then we must put on a façade, it wouldn't do to upset your mama as her health is so precarious at present.'

'As usual, my dear friend, you've provided the voice of reason. It's a shame that Patrick told you as then I wouldn't have known and therefore not been disappointed when the plans were cancelled.'

'I expect that's why he didn't involve you. Now, when exactly is Miss Parsons due to arrive? Beth is eager to meet her new companion. Did I tell you that I took all three puppies out with us and they behaved impeccably — so much so that Beth has now decided that she likes dogs after all?'

Eventually the gentlemen deigned to join them. If she hadn't known what was to happen tomorrow then she wouldn't have been aware that anything was wrong. They were both relaxed and joked and chatted as usual.

'Why don't we change for dinner tonight, my love, in honour of your mama feeling able to join us for the first time in an age.'

'Thank you, Richard, that would be a kind thing to do. Mama is always in an elaborate ensemble whatever we might be wearing. In which case Hannah and I had better go up now as it takes far longer for us to change than it does for you.'

Patrick walked with her to the door whilst the other two settled their differences. 'I know you think I don't suit black, sweetheart, so why don't I wear my regimentals? You've yet to see me in them and I'd like to impress you.'

For a second she was unable to answer and feared she would reveal that she knew his dreadful news. Then she rallied and stepped into his arms before he could retreat, thus hiding her tear-filled eyes from his inspection.

'No, much as I'd like to see you looking so splendid, dearest Patrick, you would look rather out of place. Please wear your evening garments and I'll endeavour to keep back my criticisms.'

His arms closed around her waist drawing her hard against him. She loved the feeling of her bosoms being crushed into his battle-hardened chest. She tilted her face and he obliged by kissing her.

'Enough of that, you might be betrothed but such open displays of affection will cause unnecessary comment.'

The duke's tone was stern, this wasn't a suggestion but a command. Patrick dropped his hands reluctantly and she moved away and hurried off without answering. Heaven knows what this formidable, autocratic head of the household would do if he knew her plans for tonight.

★ ★ ★

Patrick watched his lovely girl leave knowing that when she got up tomorrow he would have gone, quite possibly for ever. He thanked God, not something he did often, that things hadn't progressed any further between them and that the only woman he would ever love could now marry the doctor and have a good life without him.

Richard had the sense not to touch him or offer any comment as he walked past. 'My study, we both need a drink or two to get through tonight.'

'Forgive me, I'm going for a walk to clear my head. I know I'm doing the right thing but it's tearing me apart and I'm not good company at present. I always said that love isn't for a soldier — that worrying about anything apart from killing the enemy is a distraction.' Angrily he brushed his sleeve across his eyes. 'Look at me, I'm unmanned by my feelings for Hannah. The thought that she will move on eventually and marry Peterson is like to kill me if a Frenchie doesn't get there first.'

'Don't give up hope, your plan's a sound one. I'm going to write a letter to Wellington myself and you can take that with you. I'm certain that Hannah will wait for you. Only if you're forced to re-enlist and then get killed in action would she even contemplate another offer however beneficial it might seem.'

He nodded, unable to speak, and swung round and strode across the terrace and down into the ornamental gardens. It took him a full hour to recover his composure, to harden his heart, to be able to face what was going to be the hardest battle of his life.

* * *

They dined in formal splendour, three courses and half a dozen removes with each course, he ate what was offered but tasted none of it. The conversation was lively, the claret flowed and although he'd intended to abstain by the time the ladies rose he was feeling more relaxed.

Richard nodded to him. 'I've no wish to remain in here with you drinking port, I'd rather spend the evening with my lady.'

The duchess was an excellent pianist and performed for a while, then they played a few hands of Whist and champagne was served. He exchanged a glance with Richard who shrugged.

'I asked to have this celebratory drink served this evening, Richard, as I missed being able to congratulate Miss Westley and Mr O'Riley on their betrothal. Do you plan on having a long engagement?'

Patrick answered for them as he thought Hannah had perhaps had one too many glasses of wine with her dinner. 'Paul asked that we wait until he and Lady Sarah have returned from their wedding trip, your grace, so not until the autumn.'

'So many weddings, so much excitement, it's hardly surprising I find life here overstimulating. I shall be glad to return to the Dower House next year where I can be quieter,' the dowager duchess said.

Later coffee was served at supper time as most in this house preferred it to tea. Her grace then retired and Richard and his lady had drifted to the far side of the drawing room leaving him to spend time alone with his beloved.

'I love you, Hannah, and count myself the most fortunate fellow in the country to have you reciprocate my feelings.'

They were sitting together on a *chaise longue* and she leaned into his shoulder and he had no option but to put his arm around her.

'And I love you, Patrick, and always will. Whatever you might think to the contrary, if anything were to happen to you I'd not marry anyone else whatever the circumstances.'

He tilted her face towards him for a horrible moment thinking somehow she knew he was leaving her tomorrow but her smile reassured him. He kissed her tenderly and she responded. This wouldn't do — it wouldn't do at all.

He gently set her on her feet and then took her hand and kissed first the knuckles, and then the palm. 'I think you've had too much to drink and to be honest, so have I. Do you think you can find your own way to your bedchamber or shall I carry you as I don't think you're too steady on your feet.'

She giggled. 'I've had a lovely time, my darling, but I'm quite capable of finding my own apartment. I've become quite proficient in the saddle, shall we ride before breakfast tomorrow?'

'I've things to attend to for Richard, otherwise I'd have loved to. I shall go for

a brisk walk around the lake to clear my
head and then retire myself. Good night,
my love.'

8

Hannah wanted to run after Patrick, to tell him that she knew he was leaving the next day, but instead she hugged to herself her own secret. She had deliberately drunk two glasses of wine and another of champagne to give her the courage to do something quite scandalous.

Her maid was there to help her disrobe but was then dismissed and told not to return until the bell was rung. She could hardly credit how her life had changed this past year. In her nightgown she stood and gazed out across the grounds listening to the nightingales singing in the trees.

Her father had been a vicar in a small village and his stipend had never quite covered the family's expenses. She was the only child as her poor mama had delivered several stillborn babies before dying herself in childbed.

Papa had withdrawn into himself, but

still gave her an excellent education, and served his parishioners well. When he died there'd been nothing for her apart from the contents of the house. These she'd sold and then had had the where-withal to start looking for employment as a governess.

Despite being so young, only nineteen years of age herself, the old duke had taken a fancy to her and employed her to be companion and governess to Sarah and Amanda. Unfortunately, when he'd died so suddenly her employment had been terminated but she'd left with an excellent reference and had found a position as companion to an elderly lady.

This had been tedious in the extreme and when she'd been offered the chance to rejoin this family in whatever capacity she'd been delighted to accept. Initially she'd been employed as companion to her grace but then had become Beth's governess.

She pulled herself from her reminiscences. Dear papa would be turning in his grave if he knew what his only child was intending to do. What would she do if Patrick rejected her? Her reputation would be gone and she wouldn't have achieved her objective.

She wasn't exactly sure what took place in the marriage bed, but she'd seen farm animals mating so assumed something similar must take place between a man and his wife. She glowed all over at the thought of becoming a woman, of giving her body to the man she loved so much.

She heard a distant church clock strike midnight, the house was quiet, now was her opportunity and she must set out at once before her courage failed her. Should she unbind her hair and have it loose around her shoulders? Maybe not a good idea in case she met someone in the passageway as no well-brought-up young lady would ever be seen outside her own apartment with her hair loose.

She laughed out loud. Having her hair loose would be the least of her problems if she was seen either entering or leaving Patrick's bedroom. She would be a fallen woman, he would be her lover and she would be his mistress. Imagine that! The daughter of a vicar becoming a soldier's mistress.

With her robe on and her feet in slippers, her hair still demurely braided and hanging down the back of her neck, she thought she could bluff her way out of the situation if she was to meet anyone. She would tell them she was on her way to the kitchens as she was unaccountably in need of a soothing tisane for a headache.

Indeed, she was a little light-headed and she thought this was the result of the alcohol she'd consumed. Men went into battle the worse for drink as it gave them false courage.

There were only two sconces alight which meant one could see, but not clearly enough to read a book if one so wished.

The room she sought was the fifth door on the right. The fourth wouldn't do as that was his sitting room and she wished to step straight into his bedchamber. But did she? Would it perhaps not be better

143

to creep in through the sitting room and then approach his bedroom that way? He might still be awake and be able to stop her. However, if she did hear movement then she could wait until he fell asleep without being seen. She could hardly lurk in the corridor in her nightwear.

All the rooms, apart from the master suite where Richard and his wife slept, were identical. Slowly she turned the knob and opened the door a fraction. Silence. She slipped through and closed the door behind her. There was sufficient light from the moon outside for her to move around and avoid bumping into furniture.

His bedchamber door was ajar. She paused outside, her heart hammering so loudly she could hear it, making clarity of thought impossible. She leaned against the door frame, breathing slowly, trying to calm her nerves.

After a few minutes she pushed the door open a little more. The only sound was his even, regular breathing. Was she brave enough to go through with this or would she return to her own domain and let this moment slip through her fingers?

Her feet moved of their own volition and she was inside and moving towards the bed. Carefully she slipped her bed-robe from her shoulders and stepped out of her slippers. She wasn't at all clear if she should take off her nightgown as well but couldn't bring herself to do that. If it was to be removed then this was Patrick's task.

She was reaching round to loosen her hair when he spoke to her. Her bladder almost emptied in shock.

'Let me do that, darling girl, I've been dreaming of running my fingers through it.'

Then he was beside her, not a stitch of clothing on him, and reaching out for her. He didn't ask why she was there — that much was obvious — but more to the point he didn't tell her to go away.

With deft fingers he released the plait, then undid the ribbons at the neck of her nightgown and slid it over her shoulders so it fell to the floor. She couldn't breathe. Couldn't speak. Every touch of his fingers was like a flame running through her.

Then he picked her up and they were naked in bed together. 'I know you're leaving tomorrow, my love, but you're not going until I'm truly yours.'

His answer was more a growl than any recognisable speech. 'If I was a gentleman I'd send you back untouched. Thank God for both of us that I'm not.'

What followed was everything she'd imagined and more. The first time had been a little uncomfortable but the second and third more wonderful than anything she'd ever thought to experience. They fell asleep eventually, exhausted and content, but she woke after a couple of hours and sat up to watch him sleep for a few minutes knowing she might never have this opportunity again.

Hastily she donned her dicarded nightclothes and left him sleeping. She returned to her own bed and despite her joy at their lovemaking she cried herself to sleep.

* * *

Patrick stretched out a hand but she was gone. Hannah had left in the night but her scent lingered on the bedsheets. He didn't regret what happened and hoped that she didn't either. Knowing that she was his in every sense of the word just made him more determined to get out of the army and return to her.

There was a cursory knock at the door and Richard strode in. 'I thought you were leaving at dawn and got up to bid you farewell. Instead I find you lazing around in your bed.'

'I'll be down directly. Go away and let me get up in peace.'

If Hannah hadn't had the sense to return to her apartment then God knows what would have happened. He shuddered at the thought of Richard's reaction. His happiness changed to bitter remorse. He deserved to be horse-whipped for taking advantage of her. Thank God there was small chance of her having his baby — for the first time since he'd realised he was most likely incapable of fathering a child, he was pleased.

He tumbled out of bed, washed from head to toe, and was shaved and donning his hated uniform within a quarter of an hour. He had the accoutrements necessary for a serving non-commissioned soldier and these were in his worn and battered knapsack. The most essential of these were his tin mug, plate and knife. Without them he couldn't eat. Other more personal items he put in his saddlebags. He hesitated than shoved in civilian garments, he might just need them. He picked up the letter he'd written to Hannah and was in two minds whether to leave it or not as it was now redundant.

Richard would be suspicious if he didn't give it to him after having said he would; he knew that Hannah would understand that it had been written before they'd shared his bed. He'd only been living in this apartment for a few days but already it felt like home and he regretted leaving it so abruptly.

He had his pistol in a holster at his side and his sabre in its scabbard. His tall, black shako had seen better days but he rammed it on his head nevertheless. His white breeches were pristine and his boots were polished to a high shine.

There was a purse of gold coins tucked inside his red jacket and a handful of silver and coppers in another pocket. He stared at his reflection scarcely recognising the man who stared back at him. In that moment he understood that he was no longer a killing machine, would be useless to any officer. He wasn't soft physically, was as tough as he'd ever been, but he'd become a civilian since he and Richard had returned so suddenly from Portugal and had no desire to fight again.

Breakfast had been cooked especially for him and Richard ate as much as he did. It might be a day or more before he had the opportunity to fill his belly again.

'Take Bruno, he'll keep you safe and

get you out of trouble. Here's the letter I promised for Wellington.' Richard handed this over.

'And here's mine for Hannah. Take care of her for me, my friend, and I'll be back as soon as I can. This uniform no longer sits comfortably on my shoulders and the sooner I can discard it the better. Thank you for the horse, I'll bring him back in one piece.'

'I know you have sufficient blunt, but I want you to have this as well.' A substantial purse clinked as it dropped onto the table between them.

'Thank you, I might need it to buy my passage home. I regret not being able to assist you in the matter of Carstairs. I thought I might make arrangements whilst in London so all you have to do when he's fit is transport him there and hand him over.'

Both of Richard's ships were at sea and not expected back for months so putting the little turd on one of those was no longer possible.

'That would be helpful, but if you find

you don't have time, then I'm sure I'll manage.'

'I'll send a letter with the instructions before I sail. I'll also write again to Hannah.'

There was no more to be said and he left with a greaseproof parcel of sandwiches, as well as his flask of fresh water, pushed into his saddlebag. He cantered down the drive, didn't look back, blinking back unwanted tears.

He stayed overnight at the Red Lion in Colchester and continued with his journey the following morning. The second night he stayed in Romford and thus was able to arrive at his destination, the London docks, by mid-morning on the third day.

Arranging for transport to Spain for himself and his horse wasn't going to be simple. He made extensive enquiries and eventually discovered there was a troopship leaving the following day. He was able to obtain passage for both of them after meeting a harassed young lieutenant attempting to marshal his raw conscripts into some sort of order.

'Sergeant Major, you're a godsend. I'll happily sign the chit for you to board the same ship as us if you'll agree to temporarily serve under me and get this rabble to follow orders.'

Patrick saluted smartly. 'I'd be happy to help out, sir, but first I've an errand to run for the Duke of Denchester, he's a close friend of mine as we served together for many years before he inherited. You might have heard of Major Sinclair. He was often mentioned in dispatches.'

'I should think so — so you're the famous O'Riley? The two useless corporals can keep this lot in one place for another hour or so. Can you complete your task in that time?'

'I can, thank you, sir. Just keep them away from the brothels and the bars. You'll lose most of them if they get that far.'

He spoke to a dock labourer and he nodded enthusiastically. 'No trouble at all, your honour, we'll get this villain aboard a packet going to India. No trouble at all, sir, no trouble at all.'

The deal was struck. A guinea in advance and another when the job was done. He noted down the necessary details for the transaction to be completed successfully and then headed away from the docks and found a decent coffee shop.

He'd brought with him pen, ink and paper — this had already been addressed and franked so he could just hand it in at the nearest collection point. He scribbled a quick note to Richard and then wrote at more length to Hannah.

Dearest Hannah,

I am now about to board a ship for Spain. My intention is to deliver the letter Richard gave me to Wellington and then with all expedition return to your side.

You are my life, I want nothing more than to spend what days I have remaining at your side.

I love you and will be back to marry you at the earliest moment that I can.

It might take me some time to find

Wellington so don't expect me back until the autumn at the earliest.

Forever yours

He signed his name with a flourish, waited until the ink was dry and then folded the paper neatly. He had one of Richard's rings and he pressed the seal into the pool of melted wax. He'd done the same for the letter to his friend.

He deposited the letters and then strode back to the docks. As he walked he pushed aside all thoughts of civilian life, of being with the woman he loved, and forced his mind back into military mode. If he was to get through these next few months and achieve his goal he must become the soldier he used to be.

* * *

Amanda welcomed the new member of the household, Miss Christabel Parsons, who arrived to take up her position as companion and governess to Beth. Miss Parsons was in her thirties and her calm and relaxed manner worked perfectly with her sister. This was obviously going to be the perfect match and meant that was one worry she no longer had.

Since Patrick's abrupt departure Richard had been quiet, far more withdrawn than one would have thought a gentleman might be because his closest friend had gone away for a few months. Hannah, naturally was subdued too, but that was only to be expected as no young lady likes to be abandoned by her betrothed so suddenly.

Several days later a letter arrived for Hannah and it was from Patrick. 'Forgive me, but I'm going to read this in my apartment. I've no wish to be a watering pot in front of you.'

'At least you know he's unlikely to be in any danger. Richard assured me that there's every possibility Patrick will be able to return about the same time that Sarah and Paul get back from their wedding trip. I thought it might be pleasant for you to plan your own nuptials. Doing so will give you not only something to occupy your mind, but something to look forward to.'

'October seems a very long time away. I know that a sailor or soldier's wife must become accustomed to being apart for long periods of time. I think it would be easier to bear if we had actually been married before he left.

'If only he'd had just another two weeks before he'd had to leave then I would now be Mrs Patrick O'Riley.' With a sad smile Hannah retreated to the privacy of her own apartment no doubt to weep over the letter as she read it.

Mama, having decided she was not about to descend into mania after all, had gone to Ipswich with Paula and intended to stay overnight as there was a concert of some sort at the assembly hall that they both wished to attend.

Anyone visiting this household would be perplexed by the informality, by everyone referring to each other by their given names and not adhering to the correct procedure. Mrs Marchand, Paula, seemed uncomfortable with this so now addressed nobody by name which would be confusing if there was anyone else living here apart from herself and Richard.

There had been a letter for him from Patrick as well and, as he hadn't come to tell her its contents, she would go at once and disturb him in his study and discover what was making him so bad-tempered. He didn't look particularly pleased to see her when she wandered in without knocking. She had called out, but hadn't waited for his answer.

'I apologise if I'm disturbing you, my love, but we need to talk. I'll not leave here until whatever it is that's bothering you has been shared with me. You promised me you wouldn't keep secrets and yet I'm certain that you're doing so.'

He opened his arms and she ran into them. He held her close, kissed the top of her head and then with what sounded suspiciously like a sigh he led her to the sofa and they sat together.

'Hannah went to Patrick the night before he left. She wasn't there when I went in but I'm not blind and could see at once he'd not been alone in his bed.'

Whatever she'd expected him to reveal it hadn't been this. She did her best to appear too shocked to speak. Richard must never know Hannah had discussed this very thing with her. 'How could she have done that? More to the point, why didn't he send her away? I don't understand.'

'If you'd come to me in those circumstances, my darling, I would also have succumbed to the temptation. Patrick loves Hannah as much as I love you. What I can't comprehend is why she would risk having an illegitimate child rather than wait a few months and do things as they should be done?'

'Did you speak to him about it before he left?'

'Of course I didn't. He didn't know I knew and I was happy to leave it that way.' His smile was a trifle lopsided. 'I would have felt obliged to draw his cork at the very least and he's bigger than me.'

She smiled at his attempt at humour. Should she reveal that she'd been party to this plan? When she had agreed with Hannah that going to Patrick's room would force his hand she hadn't expected her friend to do so when she knew her betrothed was leaving.

Now there was the possiblity there would be a baby born out of wedlock. Patrick had been gone less than a week so even if Hannah was in an interesting condition she couldn't possibly know.

'I think she should marry Doctor Peterson instead . . . .'

Now he laughed out loud. 'Is that your way of preventing gossip? Devil take it, woman, the final banns for her marriage to Patrick have yet to be read and you're suggesting that she marries someone else?'

9

Hannah's hands were trembling as she broke the seal on the letter. She carefully spread out the paper and began to read. Tears trickled unheeded down her cheeks by the time she'd finished. He'd deliberately not referred to their illicit night and she was grateful for that. It was possible the duke might have opened it in error and if he knew what she'd done he would no longer wish to have her residing under his roof.

She dried her eyes and read the letter for a third time. She was being nonsensical — this was her home now and even if her secret was revealed she would be forgiven and not cast aside. She was fortunate indeed to have such friends.

She carefully put the letter with the other one she'd received and hoped that he'd have time to write on a regular basis. She couldn't reply as she'd no idea where to send it. The duke had been in low spirits since Patrick's departure and she hoped the missive he'd received would cheer him up.

There was a knock on her door and the duchess was outside. She rushed in and closed the door behind her and wasted no time with any preamble. 'My dear girl, what were you thinking of? Why couldn't you wait until Patrick returned to give yourself to him?'

'How could you possibly know?' There was no point in denying it and anyway she wasn't ashamed and had no regrets at all whatever the consequences might be.

'Richard went into Patrick's room first thing and knew at once that you'd been there.'

Hannah felt the heat travel from her toes to her crown. Her legs folded and she crumpled onto the sofa. How humiliating, how awful, to think that . . . She couldn't bring herself to ask exactly what evidence there'd been to indicate her having spent the night with her lover. Leaving as she had whilst Patrick had

been asleep had obviously not been sufficient.

'Is that why he's been so quiet? I'm
surprised he hasn't confronted me,
called me a light-skirt and asked me to
leave at once.'

Her friend reached out and squeezed
her hand. 'We're shocked, how could we
not be? But we both understand why it
happened and we must now talk about
something else. Have you considered
what you would do if you're carrying his
baby?'

'I'm not going to marry the doctor in
case you were thinking I could trick him
into making me an offer. I know I cannot stay here under those circumstances,
but I was hoping the duke might have
a small house somewhere I could go to
until Patrick comes back to marry me.

'He said in his letter that he hoped to
be home by the autumn — we could be
married immediately and then remain
isolated until after the baby came. I
know what I did was reprehensible, but I
would do it again in a heartbeat.'

'I don't think you've considered how difficult it will be if Patrick doesn't return. Your child will never be able to take his or her place in society, will forever be tainted. Is that what you want?'

'Patrick is going to return, he told me so in his letter. He loves me . . .'

'I'm sure he does, but, my dear, you must consider that he might have no choice in the matter. Wellington might refuse to release him immediately, he could be involved in fighting and be killed.'

'I've no wish to discuss this with you any longer. I thought you my friend, but everything you say points to the reverse. Would you have married someone you didn't love when there was still a very real possibility that the person you *did* love would return to you eventually?'

'Please, Hannah, I'm trying to point out the reality of the situation. Let me put it to you a different way. If Patrick was dead and you thought you might be carrying his child would you then be prepared to marry Doctor Peterson?'

'That's a hypothetical question but I can still give you my answer. It's a categorical no. I would never trick a gentleman I admire and like so shabbily. To deceive him into taking me and then foisting someone else's child on him would be, to me, a bigger sin than having a baby unwed.'

She stood up wishing to end this unpleasant conversation. 'I shall have my trunk packed and be ready to leave this afternoon. I've sufficient funds saved to rent a small cottage and to live in reasonable comfort until Patrick returns. There's no need for this family to be involved any further with either of us. I shall forward my address when I have one and would be grateful if you will send any letters from Patrick on to me.'

'If that's what you've decided, Hannah, then I'll not stop you. I'll have the carriage outside in two hours to take you wherever you want. If your maid is prepared to go with you then she may do so.'

Hannah was disappointed that her brief intimacy with her grace had ended in this way. What she didn't say was that she actually had no intention of hiding away somewhere, but intended to travel immediately to Spain and find him. They could be married by the company padre and she was confident there would be no need for banns to be called in such circumstances.

She expected at any moment to have his grace stride in and try and dissuade her from leaving but she'd completed her packing with the help of her new maid undisturbed. She wrote a polite letter of thanks to both of them, wrote another to Beth saying goodbye, and was ready to depart.

Ellie had been pleased to be offered the opportunity to accompany her so she wouldn't be entirely alone on her journey. She wasn't sure the girl would be quite so happy when she discovered where they were actually going.

She exited through the side door not wishing to draw attention to her departure. To her surprise and delight John, Patrick's valet, was waiting to hand her into the carriage.

'Her grace said I was to come with you, miss, and I'm happy to do so. Do you wish me to travel on the box?'

'No, come inside with us.' The coachman waited to be told in which direction to go and she said to head for Colchester.

She bit her lip as they drove through the gates of Radley Manor for the last time. If she hadn't gone to Patrick on his final night none of this would be happening but she still didn't regret her impulsive decision.

'Now, I've something to tell both of you. I intend to go to Spain and find my betrothed so we can be married immediately. He wouldn't take me with him but I refuse to wait at home when I don't know how long he might be away. If you don't wish to accompany me abroad then I'll give you coins for your journey back to Radley when we arrive in Colchester.'

Instead of answering John dipped into his pocket and tossed over a heavy purse. 'Her grace didn't say so in so many words, miss, but I got her drift. She said to give you this with her love and blessing.' Ellie nodded vigorously. 'I've always wanted to see the world, I'll keep you looking neat as a pin wherever we are, Miss Westley.'

★ ★ ★

Patrick soon had the recalcitrant troops in order and marched them more or less in time onto the ship and saw them stowed below. He barked his orders at the unfortunate corporals and was confident they were sufficiently in awe of him not to cause any further trouble.

Lieutenant Digby wouldn't succeed in his chosen career unless he toughened up. On the journey he would endeavour to instil some much-needed wisdom into the young man. The new troops would have had some rudimentary training before embarkation, but a junior officer had none at all and had to learn on the job.

They were fortunate that the journey was accomplished in relative comfort. Crossing the Bay of Biscay, as expected, was unpleasant but apart from that he almost enjoyed being at sea. He had the men on deck whenever possible, drilled them mercilessly in the limited space, and when they arrived in Corunna they were unrecognisable from the shambles he'd first seen milling about on the dock in London.

He'd opted to sleep with Bruno, he didn't trust a sailor to take care of his horse. He'd left his belongings in the cabin that he was supposed to be sharing with Digby. The purser sponged his jacket and he cleaned his boots so he was immaculate when they docked.

The battle had now moved well into Spain and this company of infantry was to march to join the British troops over two hundred and fifty miles away. There were three companies travelling in this ship and each had their own officer, but his was the only one to have a sergeant major as well.

He watched with some amusement as his officer parleyed with the other two equally inexperienced gentlemen. The three of them approached him.

'Sergeant Major, we've decided that it would be best for all of us if we combined our companies and put them under your command.'

Patrick hid his smile. 'I think you mean, sir, that I'm to take charge of the men whilst you and the other two officers remain in command.'

'Of course, of course, that's exactly what I meant. Go ahead, Sergeant Major.'

It didn't occur to the officers that if he was to take control of the three companies, around sixty men, then he should march with them which he had no intention of doing as he had a perfectly good horse to ride. In fact, when the mounts for the three young men were led from the hold they were distinctly inferior to his own.

They were to remain just one night in Corunna and then set out on the arduous trek to join the rest of Wellington's army. As always, in a port that shipped troops in and out, there were hostelries used exclusively by officers and those by the non-commissioned. The poor buggers in their new, hot, uncomfortable uniforms were herded into the nearest open space and told to bivouac.

There were no tents, no cooking utensils and if he didn't step in and get them organised they would go hungry. He used some of his largesse to buy the necessary pots and skillets so each company could set up their own temporary camp kitchen.

'Here, corporal, you seem to have your wits about you. Find a couple of men capable of building a fire that won't burn down the nearest buildings. Then get water from the pump and get a brew on. They have their irons, and once food is prepared they can eat. Something to put in the stewpot will arrive and only the companies ready to receive it will get any.'

Although they were to march as one unit it was better that they camped separately and got to know each other as almost certainly they would be separated when eventually they arrived at their destination. He spread more of his blunt amongst the locals and headed for his own dinner satisfied his men, as long as someone could cook, would be well-fed tonight. They couldn't march on an empty stomach. Bread, fruit and cheese had also been added to the vegetables and meat he had paid for.

There were only half a dozen sergeants in his temporary accommodation. He introduced himself and was immediately aware that they recognised his name. He wasn't sure if that was going to be of benefit to him or not.

Over a decent dinner, and large quantities of rough red wine, he discovered what was happening with Wellington's army. After winning a minor victory at Fuentes de Onoro, wherever that was,

171

the army were laying siege to the fort of Ciudad Rodrigo taken from the Spanish, and presently occupied by Marshal Ney's VI Corps.

If there was one thing Patrick hated, it was siege warfare. Inevitably there would be a forlorn hope — volunteers hoping to get promotion and extra pay by attempting to enter the besieged city through a breach in the walls. Very few of them survived, that was for sure.

'What's the best route for me to take my boys?'

'Well, I ain't been there myself. I'm stationed here taking care of the new arrivals and such,' a stout, scruffy individual replied.

'What about you, Matthews, can you be of more help?'

'What you want is a good guide, then you don't need to worry about directions.'

Patrick bit back a snarled reply. He took a deep breath and tried again. 'We've got a guide, we'd hardly set out without one. What I want to know is which towns we're likely to go through so, one, I can send ahead to make arrangements for the men, and two, I can then be sure we're not being led astray.'

Corporal Bevan had been listening to this exchange. 'I'm just back from there, Sarge, been sent to collect the mail. You go through Lugo, Astorga and then follow the river Esla the rest of the way. If you can delay your departure for a couple of days I'll be happy to return with you. I speak a bit of the lingo, which helps with the locals.'

'Thank you, Corp, that solves the problem. I'll let my officer know the change of plan.' Nobody thought this an odd thing to say — a company sergeant always knew better than a junior officer. They wouldn't have achieved this rank without having been serving King and Country for a decade.

He returned to his billet having been unable to give Lieutenant Digby the news that they wouldn't be leaving at first light after all. All three of the young gentlemen were drunk as wheelbarrows.

He'd found pen and paper and left a note in a prominent position.

When the bleary-eyed lieutenants staggered from their beds the following morning he was already drilling the three companies. By the time they set out for the fort they would be in better shape, so the delay was beneficial for all of them.

Digby, blinking and rubbing his eyes in the bright sunshine, approached him a trifle unsteadily. 'I say, Sergeant Major, they look a lot smarter than they did. As we're not to leave until the day after tomorrow I'll leave you in charge. You can send me another note at my billet if needs be.'

He watched, grim-faced, as the man who would have these poor men's lives in his hands strolled off as if he had no responsibilities at all. This one was a killing officer, no mistake about that. His decisions would lead his men to their deaths if he couldn't knock some sense into him before he actually took charge.

★ ★ ★

Amanda wasn't looking forward to explaining to her husband that yet another member of their household had abandoned them. His reaction was harsher than she'd anticipated.

'God's teeth, why didn't you stop her? How could she be allowed to leave thinking so badly of us? I'll fetch her back. I thought better of you, Amanda.'

'Richard, if you would stop shouting at me and let me continue you will understand why I was happy to see her go. She's not going to any cottage, she's doing exactly what I would do in her circumstances, she's going after Patrick.'

She had his full attention now and he looked suitably ashamed at his rude outburst. 'I beg your pardon, sweetheart, I should have known at once there was more to this story.'

When he heard that she'd arranged for John and a maid to accompany Hannah, and made sure that there were sufficient funds for the expedition, he smiled.

'In which case, I'd better get something in place for the removal of Carstairs.

Patrick told me yesterday that our prisoner was already demanding to be released by hammering on the door.'

'Nobody will hear him where he is and John assured me that the footman and groom who remained there are quite capable of keeping that young man imprisoned until he's well enough to be sent abroad. On that subject, my dear, are you quite sure you don't wish to speak to his father? Might not he wish to say goodbye to his oldest son despite his reprehensible behaviour?'

'Good God, he's just going to work his passage to India. I'm supplying the captain with the money to pay for his return as a passenger. It will just keep him out of the way for several months, probably longer, and let the dust settle.'

'Patrick informed me that the vicar hasn't seen his son since he went up to Oxford. He spends his leisure time in hellholes in London and has no interest in his family or his benefactor.'

'In which case you're right, there's no necessity to involve Mr Carstairs. From what you say I think he'll be relieved that matters have been taken out of his hands. He might even think it's divine intervention and that his son will repent his evil ways and return a changed young man.'

'Highly unlikely, but we can but hope. This leads me to another subject entirely, my love, I've noticed that you've been quiet, unhappy even, these past weeks. Tell me, what's bothering you?'

'It's you that's been different, Richard. You've been too busy to stop and speak to me. You promised when we married that I could remain involved with the running of the estates but you've relegated me to the role of housekeeper and I'm not content with that.'

His smile, as always, made her spirits lift. 'As both Paul and Patrick are no longer residing here I should be delighted to have you work alongside me. I thought to give you the opportunity to be a lady of leisure, not something you've had for many years. I apologise if I misread the situation.'

'You did, and I should have mentioned it before. Shall we repair to your study immediately so I can get started on whatever task you have in mind?'

He'd accepted her answer without question when really her main concern was the fact that she was yet to conceive a baby with him.

10

Hannah enjoyed the two day drive to London. She got to know her travelling companions and was certain that both the duke and duchess knew exactly what she intended and were giving her their full support.

'John, you must be my man of affairs, I'd like you to have charge of not only our luggage, the arrangements for our journey, but also the two purses I have with me. Your size and demeanour should discourage anyone from attempting to rob you.'

He flicked back his jacket — he was dressed in normal apparel and looked exactly like a senior servant which he now was, of course. 'I'm armed, miss, and know how to use it. I also have a stiletto in my boot. Mr O'Riley said it was always advisable to carry a knife.'

Ellie stared open-mouhed at the weapon. 'Oh my, I hope you never have to use it. Tell me, John, why would you need a knife in your boot?'

'I can take a stone out of a horse's hoof, cut away a boot from a broken leg, use it to eat my dinner and also for protection if necessary.'

The girl was suitably impressed by this explanation as was she. 'What about the other task you were given? Have you been able to find somebody else to take care of that matter?' She was referring to the beast who'd tried to force himself on Beth.

'No need to worry on that score, miss, his grace has it organised.'

They stayed overnight in a clean, but basic, hotel reasonably close to the docks. The carriage was already on its way back so John would have to arrange for a hackney to collect them when they needed to board whatever vessel he'd been able to book passage on.

Obviously, they couldn't travel through France so would have to make the long sea voyage down the coast and dock at a place called Corunna in Spain.

She was over a week behind Patrick so had no expectation of finding him still there when she arrived.

Her man of affairs took to his new role as if born to it. Considering that he had only been a senior footman before being promoted recently to valet for Patrick, he was proving to be remarkably adaptable.

'We have berths on a ship leaving at high tide. This means we must leave here immediately and there's a hackney carriage waiting outside, miss.'

John paid what was due, organised for her trunk — which also included Ellie's few items — to be transported too, whilst all she had to do was behave like a young lady of breeding and step into the cab as if this was the most normal thing in the world.

Everything she saw was new to her and she wasn't quite sure if she was excited or terrified by this adventure. Neither John nor Ellie were apprehensive so it behove her to remain outwardly calm at least. One thing she'd learned from being employed as both governess and companion was that as long as one appeared calm, everyone around would believe that was actually the case.

Somehow she'd expected the vessel they were to travel in to be considerably larger. She looked at the small ship with some trepidation but neither of her companions appeared worried so she hid her concerns.

'I'll be bunking in the hold with the other male passengers, but you and Ellie have got a cabin. It won't be luxurious or spacious but you'll have your privacy.'

'Will we be aboard for very long? If my geography and mathematics are correct it will take quite a few days to get there even if the winds are favourable.'

'I reckon that's right, miss, anything from six to eight depending on the weather and the wind. Have you thought what we'll do when we arrive?'

'I'm assuming that knowledge of the whereabouts of Wellington's army will be easy to obtain. I'm not sure that hiring or buying a vehicle to transport us will be as simple.'

'I'll do my best to find us something suitable. We'll need an English-speaking guide as well. I can drive a carriage and take care of the horses so that's one less thing to worry about.'

'Actually I'm able to speak sufficient Spanish to make myself understood. My papa believed that all young ladies should have a knowledge of more than one foreign language. I also speak good French — but I hope that won't be needed.'

Ellie didn't know why John laughed and Hannah thought it best not to enlighten her. The only reason her French would be needed was if they were taken prisoner by Bonaparte's army.

The cabin proved to be even smaller than anticipated, barely room for the two of them to stand up at the same time. There were bunks against one wall and Ellie was happy to take the top and leave the lower one for her.

'My, miss, this is ever so small but it's put together in a clever way. As long as one of us sits with our feet out of the way on the bottom bunk there's room enough to move about.' She opened the door to a small cupboard. 'Look, a chamber pot and under this lid there's a basin. I suppose having them made out of tin is to save them getting broken in a storm.'

'I'm sure you're right, Ellie. There's space for the trunk to be pushed in neatly but it will have to be pulled out each time you wish to open the lid so please get out what we need for the next day or two to make things easier.'

'Do I have to fetch hot water or will someone bring it to us? What about the po?'

There was no time for an answer to these pertinent questions as the conversation was interrupted by a sharp tap on the cabin door. Hannah drew her legs up and Ellie scuttled past.

'Good afternoon, Miss Westley. I'm the purser and will be taking care of you. This here is Eli, cabin boy, and he'll fetch and carry for you. He's got hot water so you can freshen up. We ain't in a position to do any laundry so best make things last until we dock again.'

He stepped to one side and Eli, who looked no more than ten years of age, sidled in and placed a brightly painted metal jug on the only other surface available, a shelf that ran above the space for the trunk. There was a jug-sized indentation ready to receive it.

'You and your maid will dine with the captain, miss, Eli here will fetch you when it's time.'

'Is it permissible for us to be on deck or must we remain below? Also, can we open the porthole or must it remain closed at all times?'

'Stay below until we sail, miss, if you don't mind. A lot of toing and froing going on and there ain't much room for ladies. Portholes remain closed in case the weather changes unexpectedly. The weather's set fair for the next few days so I reckon we'll make good time.' He touched his forehead in a gesture of respect and closed the door.

'I just hope that neither of us are seasick, Ellie. I've no idea if I will find being on the water makes me cast up my accounts as I've never set foot on a boat before.'

'It's bobbing up and down a bit already, miss, but I like it, I don't think it'll upset me.'

Until her maid had pointed it out she'd not been aware of the movement beneath her feet, somehow she'd been adjusting to it without thought.

'We can't see much through this tiny window but it gives us some light. Without it this would be like being shut in a store cupboard. It's surely no bigger than that.'

The hot water was redundant but Ellie positioned the jug in a second hollowed-out circle next to the wash-stand which had obviously been made to hold it steady when the ship was in motion. John had told her this was a packet, a fast mail ship, that took a few passengers but no other cargo.

They clambered into their surprisingly comfortable berths and the rocking sent them both to sleep. They were roused by Eli banging on the door saying he'd come to take them to dinner.

She sat up and cracked her head on the upper bunk which made her feel quite sick for a moment. Ellie scrambled out of her bunk and called out to the cabin boy that they would be ready in ten minutes.

'Things are moving about a bit more now, miss, I reckon we're under way.'

Within the allotted time they were ready to be escorted the short distance to the captain's accommodation which Eli told her was in the forecastle — not the front end of the vessel as she'd referred to it.

The cabin they entered was surprisingly spacious and had a table laid up for dinner under an expanse of windows. These couldn't be called portholes as they weren't round. John was there and he moved at once to her side protectively. There were three men in naval uniform, presumably the captain and his officers, plus two other smartly dressed gentlemen of middle years.

They all seemed inordinately pleased to see that they were to be joined by ladies. She was introduced but promptly forgot the names. Dinner was three palatable courses but no removes, wine was served for the gentlemen and freshly squeezed lemonade for herself and Ellie. There was even coffee after the plates and debris had been cleared.

It was now quite dark outside and the interior was lit by oil lamps. Apart from the constant swaying underfoot one might have thought one was at a dinner party.

'Thank you for a delightful evening, captain, but if you'll excuse me, my maid and I are going to retire.'

John had drunk only two glasses of wine whereas the other gentlemen present had imbibed considerably more. One of them, a dark-visaged person wearing a violently striped waistcoat, was eyeing her in a way she wasn't comfortable with.

'I'll escort you to your cabin, miss. Good night, sirs.' John nodded politely and then placed himself at her back so that the leering man was no longer able to see her.

Despite pushing the flimsy bolt across the door Hannah didn't feel entirely safe in her small cabin.

* * *

Patrick was horrified at the ignorance of the young men supposedly in command of their company. At no time did they check that the men had food and access to fresh water. When eventually he found Wellington the first thing he would do was make a formal complaint against the three of them. He'd arranged with the quartermaster for the necessary vittles to be loaded onto a cart for the journey. The man had been happy to reimburse him for what he'd spent from his own pocket.

'Good thing there's men like you returning to serve, those three nincompoops would have let the men starve without your intervention.'

'Have they applied for the necessary

funds to replenish our food stocks?'

'No, I reckon I'll give it to you. From what I've seen and heard the three of them would drink it away before you'd even set off. Shocking bad example to the men.'

'There are good officers and then there are the ones we've got here. Hopefully, whoever the brigade commander is will soon put things right.'

God knows why they'd chosen a career in the military as they obviously had no interest in their duties. The following two nights they not only got drunk they also brought in prostitutes from the local brothel to the officers' accommodation. If there'd been anyone more senior present this would have been stopped but unfortunately they were the only ones there.

He routed out the men at dawn and drilled them for two hours whilst it was still cool. Not only would it improve their ability to fight it should also help their new boots to soften and make it easier to walk the two hundred and fifty miles. An experienced column of men could cover more than twenty miles in a day and still be fit enough to fight. He thought it highly unlikely these would be able to do more than fifteen. This meant it was going to take more than two weeks to complete the journey and that's if there were no disasters or interruptions.

He wrote two letters to Hannah and one to Richard just to occupy his time. As they were waiting for the mail packet to turn up it made sense to add his letters to the bags being returned to England. He'd become better acquainted with Corporal Bevan and spent his evenings in his company.

During their enforced delay Patrick discovered that Bevan collected and delivered the mail with a diligence pulled by two heavy horses. He also had two soldiers to guard the contents.

'It was a stroke of good fortune to find you waiting here. It will speed up our march considerably as any of the men unable to continue can not only travel on our diligence but also with you.' He didn't ask for permission — after all he outranked this young man. 'I'm expecting there to be some that suffer from heat exhaustion or bloody feet and I don't want them to slow us down or fall by the wayside.'

'It's devilish hot by mid-morning and remains so until five o'clock.'

'I was aware of that, young man. My intention is to get the men up before dawn to breakfast and then to march them until around eleven o'clock. I'll send my officer ahead to find somewhere in the shade they can rest.'

'Useless lot of buggers they've sent us this time, pardon me for saying so, Sarge. It's more like to be them that collapse than any of the men. It's a bleedin' disgrace, that's what it is.'

Patrick agreed with every word but could hardly say so. 'I'll forget you said that, Bevan. I'm going to check on Bruno and then get some shut-eye.'

He also wished to make sure that all the men were settled, that none of them had wandered off to the brothel or imbibed an excessive amount of alcohol. Walking for hours in hot sunshine after a night of heavy drinking would make things worse for them.

He'd set sentries to watch the perimeter of the camp and they did their job efficiently and demanded his name and rank. He walked around the three camps stopping to talk, knowing most of their names by now so he was able to address them personally. Satisfied all sixty soldiers were accounted for and all were content he headed to the stables.

He'd forgotten how much he'd enjoyed the rapport he'd once had with the men, the comraderie of communal living, the way strangers could meld into a tight-knit unit just by drilling and living together. Perhaps he'd been too quick to dismiss a return to his career as a soldier. Civilian life was pleasant but held no excitement and he would always be beholden to Richard; whereas now he was his own man. Then an image of Hannah filled his head. If he re-enlisted he would lose her and he wasn't prepared to do that.

He pushed these thoughts aside as he had a job to do and his personal life must come second to his responsibilities to those under him.

* * *

He had the men lined up at dawn, Corporal Bevan and his two companions were ready to depart, the wagon with the belongings of the officers, as well as the necessary rations and barrels of water, was also waiting. He'd sent one of the corporals to wake the three lieutenants an hour ago so where the hell were they? The lieutenants's luggage was already loaded and all they had to do was put the few personal items they had in their bedchamber into saddlebags and even those three could manage that.

He dropped the reins in front of Bruno knowing he would remain where he was and marched into the inn where they were living. Being so early there were no maids or potboys cleaning up the wreckage from the previous night — but more worryingly, the place was silent.

He had two sensible choices. The first was to go up and tip the three of them in turn from their beds and risk a court martial. The second, to knock politely on the door and then hang about waiting for them to appear in their own good time. Neither of these appealed to him.

There was a third option. He would set out without them, leave them a note giving them the direction they should take when they eventually got up. With any other young officers he would hesitate to jeopardise their position with the men by doing this. These three treated him as if he was their superior and not the reverse, so he was confident he'd get away with it.

He wrote the note and then shoved it under the door. He banged on it for good measure but didn't risk telling them what he intended in case one of them was sufficiently awake to remember that he was an officer and insist that the companies remained where they were.

★ ★ ★

Predawn was perfect for marching and Patrick thought they could complete more than ten miles before they needed to find shelter from the sun. All the men had a water flask at their hip and could refresh themselves as they walked. They'd arrived with the hated leather stocks but he'd given them permission to remove these and stow them carefully in their knapsacks to be replaced when they arrived. They chafed the neck and some commanding officers were old-fashioned and would insist their men wore the leather regardless of the discomfort it gave them.

He positioned the mail wagon at the front of the column and the other at the rear. They were making good progress and so far no one was flagging but all keeping in reasonable step. They weren't expected to march as they would in a drill but it helped to have them all walking at the same pace.

He cantered up to the guide who

was riding a remarkably handsome Arab — his must be a lucrative profession nowadays.

'I'm going to need somewhere in the shade in a couple of hours where the men can cook and rest until dusk. We'll then continue for a further couple of hours before bivouacking. Do you know of anywhere suitable?'

'There is, Señor, other troops have used it. We should arrive before the sun's too hot.'

There was still no sign of the young gentlemen and it was a good two hours since they'd set out. Surely the lazy devils would be out by now and on their way? If they didn't arrive before the march was halted there would be ample opportunity for them to catch up whilst they rested for several hours.

It wasn't until late afternoon, the sun at its zenith, that the missing officers joined them. 'I say, Sergeant Major, what a lark. Can't believe how far you've come. Well done.' Lieutenant Digby dismounted looking none the worse for having ridden in the heat for several miles. The horses, however, were sweat-stained and thirsty.

He was about to issue orders to the nearest soldiers to walk the beasts until they were cool, but for all their disregard of the needs of their men, these three immediately took care of their own mounts. He was happy to share his tasty stew and tea with them when they eventually joined him.

'We remain here until it's cooler, sir, then march for another two hours before setting up camp. The horses will be rested and fed by then as well.'

'Is it usual, Sergeant Major, to abandon your officers as you did?'

'It isn't, sir, but I believed you would prefer us to set off as soon as we could. These troops are needed and any delay will be frowned upon. As you are mounted I knew you'd catch us up easily.'

'That's what we thought. Thinking of the men's welfare as usual. We have full confidence in you.'

11

Hannah was woken by a loud thud as something heavy crashed into the cabin door. She hadn't undressed completely, was in her undergarments, and rolled out of her narrow bunk, staring at the door apprehensively.

'There's somebody out there, miss, what shall we do?'

'I'm not sure, I think it might be that man who was leering at me over dinner. I don't think the bolt will hold.'

There were several further thumps and then to her astonishment John called out cheerfully. 'Nothing to worry about, miss, the unwanted visitor has been dealt with.'

She rushed to the door and spoke through it. 'Is it that man?'

'It is. I remained out here just in case he tried his luck. Two of the sailors have taken him away and he'll not bother you again. Good night, Miss Westley, good night, Ellie.'

Hannah remained where she was until his footsteps faded. 'Thank goodness he stood guard. I'm glad he didn't have to shoot him as that might have been difficult to explain to the captain.'

They returned to their berths and she found the rocking motion soothing and was soon deeply asleep and didn't wake again until Eli banged on the door.

'I've got your hot water, miss, and I'm to take your po and empty it. I'll leave the water and come back in a minute for the other.'

She remained where she was whilst her maid dealt with the unpleasant task of conveying the full receptacle to the door and then placing it outside.

'It's ever so noisy out there now. I reckon they're putting sails up and down and such. Can we go up and look?'

'I think it better if we wash and dress first, Ellie. The motion of the ship seems more violent now. I do hope we're not in for a storm.'

'If you look out of the window it's ever

so sunny and nice and there's no big waves at all.'

★ ★ ★

So the pattern of her days was established. They took their meals with the other passengers but only saw the captain and his officers at dinner. Fortunately, nobody enquired after the absent gentleman and she found everybody else respectful and charming.

Being on deck was quite wonderful even though crossing the Bay of Biscay was decidedly bumpy. They completed the run down the French coast in excellent time and on the sixth day sailed into Corunna. She'd never thought to travel and yet here she was, without a gentleman to take care of her apart from John, about to set foot on foreign soil.

John had a leather satchel over his shoulder with his belongings contained within it. Her trunk was of moderate size and neatly bound with leather straps. This made it easier to transport.

Knowing it would be hot in Spain she'd only brought lightweight gowns and one cloak in case the weather was inclement.

They disembarked too late to continue their journey that day but John found them decent lodgings and they then sat down together to a tasty dinner. Eating with one's servants would be unheard of in England but she stood on no ceremony as after all she was little more than a servant herself.

'I find it extraordinary that dinner is eaten so late by the Spanish. I suppose we'll have to adapt to their routine in future.'

'You being able to speak the lingo, miss, made things a deal easier,' John said as he finished the last mouthful of a tasty rice and fish stew. 'I'm going to go in search of a carriage and guide, miss, and whilst I'm out I'll discover exactly where the British army is. Do you wish me to enquire after Mr O'Riley?'

'Sergeant Major O'Riley, John. Yes, that would be helpful as we would then know how far ahead of us he is.'

'He's got Bruno. I doubt we'll catch up before he gets to Wellington, but you never know, something might delay him.'

On that cheerful note he excused himself and went about his business. She decided to write to her grace as she'd been told that post would be taken by any ship that was returning to England. The landlady explained that a letter could be handed over at an inn near the port and the postage would be paid there.

Ellie was reluctant to go out with the letter on her own. 'I don't know what they're saying to me, miss, it's not natural. They should speak English like proper Christians.'

'No doubt they think the same of us. They might be Roman Catholics, but they're still Christians. We shall go together. I know we don't have John with us but it won't be dark for an hour or two. The Señora said it was perfectly safe for ladies to walk about on their own in daylight.'

On the walk back to their lodgings John joined them. 'I've good news on both fronts, Miss Westley. It was cheaper to buy a carriage and hire a guide than to hire them both. I've got a barouche, so let's hope it don't rain. There's a canopy that'll keep you shaded. I bought two decent nags to pull it.'

'Oh, well done. What did you find out about Wellington?'

'Now, that's not so good news. He's blooming miles away. Two hundred and fifty or thereabouts.'

'Goodness me, that will take us much more than a week to accomplish. What did you learn about Patrick?'

'He's already met up with some troops. He'll not travel as fast as we will and with luck we'll overtake him before he gets there. He left Corunna ten days ago.'

'I do hope so. Finding him in a vast encampment might prove diffcult.'

'We need to leave before dawn, get some miles in early as it gets too hot to travel after eleven o'clock.'

'I take it there was no language difficulty, that our guide speaks English?'

'Enough, miss. Seems a good sort of cove. I'll be waiting outside with the carriage tomorrow. I've settled the account for the accommodation.'

★ ★ ★

The first town of any size that they would reach was called called Lugo and there they'd be able to spend the night in reasonable comfort. It appeared that until they arrived at a place called Astorga their accommodation would be primitive at best and non-existent at worst. The distance between the two towns was over one hundred miles. John thought they would be fortunate to travel thirty miles in a day.

'A stagecoach travels at eight or nine miles an hour, John, surely even on these tracks we should be able to do five or six.'

'I reckon we might, miss, but remember we can't be out in the heat of the day which means only six hours on the road. We have to let the horses rest or they'll

205

not make the journey.'

'How fast do you think the soldiers will be able to walk?'

'Not more than three miles an hour, I reckon, which means we'll make up the time nicely.'

John had thought of everything and on the empty seat in the vehicle were the necessities for camping overnight. He'd also packed cooking utensils, cutlery, plates and a variety of beans and other food items. She was determined look upon this as an adventure and not something to be dreaded.

Her ability to converse in Spanish even at a basic level made things so much easier. The villagers were delighted to find an English lady who could speak to them in their own tongue and were most hospitable. They were invited into farmhouses to sleep and had no need to overnight in the open on this part of the journey.

The heat was draining and after a few days she'd abandoned her heavy petticoats and corset and was now travelling in a plain grey gown that she'd once used as a governess. She thought that she and Ellie were indistinguishable now from their appearance, but somehow no one mistook her for the servant.

On the fifth day they were approaching Astorga and she was looking forward to being able to wash her hair and her person with more thoroughness than she'd been able to so far. Every part of her was grimy and she did so hate not being clean.

One thing this journey had demonstrated quite clearly to her was that she wasn't really cut out to be a soldier's wife. Following the drum was not for her — what she would do if Patrick had been obliged to re-enlist she'd no idea.

That night her monthly courses came and she began to think that her impetuous adventure had been a dreadful error of judgement. She could hardly turn back now having come so far but wished with all her heart that she hadn't left the comfort and cleanliness of Radley Manor.

★ ★ ★

Patrick got to know the officers and began to revise his initial opinion about their suitability. It was more ignorance than anything else that had caused them to behave so badly. They had all been recently promoted from ensigns having spent their first few months in Colchester supposedly learning the basics of command, but in fact spending most nights getting roaring drunk.

They were all from wealthy and titled families, hence the rapid and undeserved promotion, but as second and third sons they had no inheritance to speak of so must make their own way in the world.

They passed through two small towns but didn't seek accommodation in either. He sent two of the corporals in to buy fresh produce and several skins of wine. The men would probably prefer ale but there was none to be had. One week into their march and they'd noticeably improved under his tutelage and were gradually learning how to control their troops.

'How far have we come, Sergeant Major?' Lieutenant Digby asked one evening as they were sitting around his campfire. Officers didn't as a rule mingle with other ranks but these three congregated with him most nights eager to hear his stories and garner whatever knowledge they could before joining a regiment.

'Close to one hundred and twenty five miles by my reckoning. If we're able to keep up this pace we should be there in between a week to ten days.'

'Good show. I think the men have settled into a routine. I'm not sure they enjoy being drilled for an hour during our rest period.'

'They need to be able to form rank and square, load and fire smoothly as if it was second nature to them. It will save their lives when it comes to battle.'

Corporal Bevan had appointed himself orderly to the gentlemen and between them they'd eliminated the excessive drinking and the officers were beginning to look more as they should. Whoever inherited them would be grateful for his input. Bevan poured them all another mug of coffee.

'Your time in India with Major Sinclair, I beg your pardon, his grace, was something I'd like to have experienced myself. Mind you, I'm not sure I'd have enjoyed the heat. I'm finding Spain quite hot enough for me, I can tell you,' Digby said as he slurped. 'This would taste a damn sight better with a slug of brandy in it. I don't suppose you have any?'

'I don't, sir, and you finished the last bottle two days ago,' Bevan lied smoothly.

'It's damn cold in the winter here, especially in the mountains,' Patrick said as he stood up. 'Excuse me, sirs, I need to check the lines before getting some shut-eye.'

'I'll see to Bruno for you. He's a magnificent animal — I don't suppose you want to sell him?'

'No, not mine to part with. His grace has loaned him to me.'

Bevan joined him as he strolled around

the encampment. They'd become good friends over the past few days. 'Have you decided what you're going to say to his lordship?'

'I think it more likely that it will be what he says to me that will matter. It depends how things are going with the siege. I'm not much use to him under those circumstances but if they breach the walls he might well want me. I'm a fighting man and experienced in battle.'

'Only officers are mounted so you might find your fine steed removed from your care.'

'That might well have been the case if the horse belonged to me. I have the papers in my pocket proving his provenance and that the Duke of Denchester intends that I return him at some point. If they wish to buy him they'll have to contact my friend.'

He enjoyed sleeping under the stars, had done so on numerous occasions, and had no difficulty settling. The men had grumbled at first but were now accustomed to this existence. Most of them had come from the deprivation of a life in the slums of London and were now, for the first time, fed, clothed and had some structure to their lives.

He suspected a dozen or more of the men had been given the option of enlisting or being tossed into prison for a variety of misdemeanours. As long as they followed orders and were brave in battle nobody gave a damn where they'd come from originally.

The encampment rose before dawn and the men were ready to march an hour later. Occasionally someone in the ranks began to sing or play the penny whistle and others joined in. As he didn't object neither did the officers.

They were climbing steadily through high ground, steep cliffs on either side of the track. It was cooler here but hard work for the men. He rode ahead and found the perfect place to make camp and rest until the heat was more bearable. The contrast at night would be noticeable and they would need more than the cooking fire to keep warm. For the first time the men would be grateful to have heavy uniforms and a greatcoat rolled up and strapped to their knapsacks.

He approached his officer and saluted. 'Sir, two miles ahead there's a clearing in the shade of the cliffs and fresh water available. There's also grazing for the horses. Do I have your permission to halt the march an hour earlier today?'

'You do, you know the men better than I do. I can hardly credit how every last one of them has managed to walk so far without complaint and with only minor injuries to their persons.'

'Once the companies are attached to a brigade they'll have to travel more quickly than this. The army marches as fast as circumstances demand — they might well also have to march overnight and then fight in the morning. This is by way of a gentle introduction.'

'I would have insisted we travelled more quickly if there'd been any urgency. These three companies will not be essential to a siege.'

'That's correct, sir. Excuse me, I'll

inform the corporals of your orders.'

Naturally enough being told they were to halt an hour earlier than usual was received with cheers. Patrick, after his initial reservations about returning to army life, was enjoying himself. Every day was different, his judgement and experience were needed. Hannah was forgotten until he was curled up under his greatcoat looking at the stars.

They covered the short distance in record time and soon the makeshift camp was established, the men took it in turns to refill their water flasks with the cold, mountain water, and the appetising smell of roasting goat drifted from the campfires making his mouth water.

Bruno and the other three horses were contentedly grazing on the lush grass that grew around the stream. He was sitting with his back against a cartwheel drinking tea and eagerly anticipating his midday meal. The bread purchased the day before would still be palatable if toasted on the end of a bayonet. The cool breeze was refreshing and all was well in his new world.

Suddenly Bruno raised his head, his ears pricked forward and he whinnied, the sound echoing around the space. He was on his feet and heading for the horses before anyone else had reacted.

'What's wrong, old fellow?' He'd heard that there were wildcats, lions and wolves up here in the hills and this would be the perfect place for one of them to pounce on an unwary horse. He couldn't smell anything untoward. Then, faintly, he heard the sound of horses approaching. He shouted orders and the men were on their feet, their muskets ready to be loaded in seconds.

Lieutenant Digby was at his side his eyes wide with apprehension. There was no sign of the other two young gentlemen. 'Is it the French? Spanish partisans? Are we going to be attacked?'

★ ★ ★

'I think we should get out and walk, Ellie, it's becoming quite steep and it's not fair on the horses,' Hannah said.

John twisted round from his position on the box. 'If you don't mind doing so, miss, it will help.'

He didn't get down to help them out, they were both now practised at clambering from the barouche without assistance.

'It's ever so pretty up here, miss, like something in one of those books you showed me in the schoolroom.'

'And so much cooler too. We'll let the carriage go ahead at its own pace and we can stroll along behind it. At least we don't need a parasol as we can walk at the edge of the track close to the cliff and hence be in the shade.'

The carriage vanished around the bend in the track half a mile ahead leaving them alone. Initially she thought it eerily silent but then, as her ears adjusted, she could hear birds of prey calling to each other high up in the sky. The guide had said they were eagles. Imagine that!

When she returned to the comfort of England she would have these memories and so, for that reason, was glad that she'd made this journey.

When they rounded the corner the barouche was stationary. John must be waiting for them to catch up. Her stomach roiled as he was suddenly surrounded by soldiers. For a moment she couldn't make sense of what she was seeing. Then Patrick appeared looking magnificent in his uniform. For some reason the red of his jacket didn't clash with the red of his hair.

She was running without realising she'd increased her pace. He was moving even more swiftly in her direction. She forgot her reservations and threw herself into his waiting arms.

12

Amanda handed the letter she'd received from Hannah over to Richard to read. He scanned the neat writing and nodded.

'It seems she's not so far behind Patrick that she won't be able to catch up with him before he reaches Wellington. I noticed two letters came for her from him — I suppose there's little point in sending them back again.'

'Hardly. What did Patrick have to say?' When she heard that he'd already established himself as a competent and experienced soldier she was concerned.

'Why do you look so bothered, sweetheart? Surely it's better that he slips back into his role, travels at the army's expense, than otherwise?'

'I know that you were reluctant to take up your duties and title last year when you arrived. However, you changed your mind and apparently were happy to be in

218

such a privileged position. Now I think you envy him. You find life here tedious and not to your taste.'

'God's teeth, why would you say such a thing? There's been nothing but excitement this past year. In the past few months I've galloped across the country-side to rescue Patrick from the Provost Marshals, done so again to collect your mother, and married you. Then there was the excitement with Sarah and Paul and now this business with Carstairs. Hardly a week goes past without something out of the ordinary occurring.'

'Which reminds me, Doctor Peterson went to see your prisoner this morning and reports that he is now able to use his jaw. He tried to escape, had to be restrained by the servants, and is threatening all sorts of things against the family for imprisoning him.'

'Then I'll speak to him. I asked Peterson to leave sufficient laudanum to knock Carstairs out so we can transport him to the docks. Did he give it to you?'

'I locked it in your desk drawer, my

love. I own I'll be delighted when this particular excitement is over. The one person one would expect to be damaged by the encounter is Beth, but she's quite forgotten what happened so Miss Parsons was telling me earlier.'

She played for him until it was time to retire. There could be no lovemaking tonight as she had her monthly courses, much to her disappointment. This time she'd really thought she might be increasing as she'd felt nauseous first thing and her bosom was tender to the touch. Paula had told her these were quite often the early symptoms of pregnancy. Of course, the only certain way to know was when one's courses had stopped coming for three months.

As always at these times she slept in her own apartment thus indicating to him that she wasn't available. What use was she if she couldn't provide him with an heir? How would she remain cheerful when inevitably Sarah was in an interesting condition? Also, quite possibly Hannah was already expecting too.

For the first time since her marriage she was unhappy. Mama, since the arrival of her companion, was no longer interested in her daughters, even Beth rarely got any of her attention. Having returned from Ipswich she'd then set out for Bath for an extended stay taking a retinue of staff with her.

Radley Manor no longer felt like home. It was too big, not furnished or decorated to her taste, and she decided that as soon as that wretched Carstairs was gone she would remove herself back to the Dower House. She wouldn't mind what dust and noise there might still be from the construction of what would be the new Denchester family home.

She fell asleep happier than she'd been for some time. Having something to plan for, something of her own to do, gave her a purpose in life once more. She would inform Richard they were moving once the house had been brought back into order.

★ ★ ★

'Hannah, what the hell are you doing here? I didn't think to see you again so soon.' Much to the enjoyment of the watching soldiers he swept her up and kissed her.

'I'll explain everything to you later, Patrick. You were right, you look wonderful in uniform.'

He kept his arm around her waist as he escorted her into the clearing under the cliffs. John grinned as he expertly manoeuvred the carriage off the track. The fact that she was here and accompanied by his valet and her maid must mean that Richard had sanctioned this extraordinary journey.

'I must introduce you to my senior officers.' Before he could do this Bruno barged into them almost knocking her from her feet in his delight to see someone from home. This was odd as Hannah had only started to frequent the stables recently.

'I'm pleased to see you too, silly boy. Are these your friends?' The officers' horses had come over to see what the fuss was about and she was unbothered by being surrounded by so many equines. This gave him a few moments to marshal his thoughts and also to watch the woman he loved.

Despite being dressed in a plain, grey gown she looked, to him, the most beautiful woman in the world. From the admiring glances she was getting not only from the men but also from the lieutenants he wasn't the only one to appreciate her.

Lieutenant Digby grabbed his arm. 'I say, Sergeant Major, you didn't say that your young lady was joining you. I thought one had to have permission from one's commanding officer for such a thing to happen.'

'I don't have one to ask permission from, and I didn't know that Miss Westley, my betrothed, intended to follow me. Allow me to introduce you.'

Hannah emerged from the circle of horses and didn't curtsy but merely nodded and kept her hand firmly at her side so the over-enthusiastic young gentleman had no opportunity to kiss it. She was every inch a lady of quality and if he was still amazed that such a jewel had chosen him, then it was hardly surprising that three actual gentlemen found the whole thing quite astonishing.

John set up a table and two stools as if they were having a picnic in a grand park and not situated somewhere in the wilds of Spain. Hannah disappeared behind the carriage with her maid no doubt to wipe the grime from her face and hands before joining him. This gave him the opportunity to talk to his man.

'I'm glad that you're here, John, I can see that Miss Westley has been well looked after. How long after my departure did you set out?'

'Six days, sir, and we had a fast crossing and no problems following you. Her grace sanctioned this expedition and funded it too.'

'It would appear that I'm to be a married man rather sooner than I anticipated. Will you stand up for me? We should arrive in Benavente tomorrow and I need you to find a padre of some sort so we can tie the knot before we continue.'

John glanced over his shoulder before speaking to ensure that they weren't overheard. 'It's like this, Sergeant Major, I think that Miss Westley might have changed her mind about becoming a soldier's wife. She's not enjoying travelling and has mentioned to Ellie several times that she can't wait to return to England.'

As Patrick had already come to the same conclusion why did this news strike him like a fist in the chest? 'In which case, I'll talk to her and then, when things are settled, she can return to England if she so wishes.' He didn't say that the engagement would be severed, but this was implied and John understood.

They wouldn't be resuming their journey for another three hours so there was ample time to have a quiet conversation and see how the land lay. They ate the stew, drank the tea, and then John and Ellie removed the remains and left them alone.

'Why did you follow me, Hannah?'

'The duke knew that I'd been at your side all night and told her grace. She suggested that I marry the doctor just in case I was expecting. I decided to follow you instead.' She fiddled with her sleeve and then looked up. 'I'm not with child so am not sure if we should get married so precipitously.'

'We have no choice, my love. You shouldn't return unmarried as your reputation will be gone. Are you having second thoughts about marrying me?' This wasn't the right thing to say as he'd just told her she had no choice but to marry him. Instead of waiting for her answer he continued deciding to explain what he'd decided.

'I like being a soldier, I hadn't realised how much I'd missed it. I thought I'd finished with the military life and the fact that they were trying to manipulate me into re-enlisting just made me more determined to refuse.

'However, I've now made up my mind that I'll do as they want. We could get married but then you can return as my wife and live comfortably . . . '

'You will remain here possibly for years and could be killed.'

'That's true. I've realised that I don't want to be dependent on someone else for my livelihood. I've got prize money invested and it's more than enough for us to pay our own way. With luck I'll add to it substantially over the next few years.'

'I wanted to have children of my own but you're denying me that. Let me get this quite clear in my mind. You came here with the intention of getting released and then returning to me. Now that's changed and regardless of my wishes you intend to be a soldier again.'

'You told me you wanted to follow the drum, you have travelled over a thousand miles to find me. I'm not the only one to have reconsidered.' This wasn't going well. What should have been a joyful reunion was turning into a disaster.

'I won't marry you, Patrick. I understand now that loving someone isn't enough to make a successful union. I've no wish to be married to a man who considers killing for a living preferable to being with me and raising a family.'

They were speaking quietly and no one would be aware that with every word spoken their relationship was disintegrating. 'I have to tell you something else which will make this easier for both of us. I cannot father children.

'You would be better off with Peterson, you will live a life of luxury, produce a nursery full of little ones. I can give you none of those things. You're right to say that loving someone isn't enough. I think very few unions are fortunate enough to have strong feelings between the partners.'

'Then I release you from our engagement, Patrick. Thank you for being so honest. I don't enjoy being uncomfortable and dirty, travelling abroad is not for me. I'd make you an appalling wife. I wish you well in your endeavours and will always hold you in my heart.'

She stood up and nodded politely as

if to a stranger. It was hard to credit that little more than two weeks ago she'd been naked at his side. She was right to sever the connection. The fault was on his side as he should have sent her away when she'd come to him.

He would never love another woman, never marry now, and it would kill him to think of her with another man.

'And I wish you well, sweetheart. I know it might not seem like it but it's a good thing you came as it has made things clearer for both of us. Excuse me, I'll speak to John and make arrangements for your departure.'

★ ★ ★

Hannah didn't talk to Patrick again. She watched him moving about the camp speaking to his men, more at ease here than she'd ever seen him in England. He was right. Life without children would be miserable indeed and she bitterly regretted her impulsive decision to give herself to him.

Only the duke and duchess knew of her assignation that night and she was certain they'd never reveal this to anyone. If they set out tonight for Corunna they could be back at the port within a week and with any luck get a packet back to London.

Nobody need know where she'd been, especially if she spent the remainder of the summer at Margate or somewhere similar enjoying the sea and entertainments offered there. It would be thought highly unconventional for a young lady of her age to be unchaperoned but that bothered her not one jot.

She would return in October to live with her friends and decide then whether her wish to have a family of her own would compensate for marrying a man that she didn't feel more than affection for. One thing was quite certain, most marriages amongst the gentility were arranged to benefit one party or the other. Quite possibly the partners disliked each other initially but somehow learned to live together in some harmony.

If Doctor Peterson offered for her she would give it serious consideration. He would never make her heart beat faster, never lift her spirits in the same way that Patrick did, but he was a good man and possibly she might come to love him eventually.

The young officers avoided her company and she and Ellie rested in the carriage until it was time to begin their trek back to the coast. At five o'clock as it got cooler the soldiers fell into ranks, the first cart set off. Patrick astride Bruno left at the head of the column and the three officers slotted in at the rear. The baggage cart trundled off and soon all she could see was a cloud of dust.

'We need to leave immediately, miss, if we're going to find somewhere to stay tonight. I'll harness the horses and then we can go.' John set about his business and two hours later the guide led them into little more than a hamlet.

He rode alongside the carriage and explained to her that this was where his wife's family lived. They could find lodgings there. This was the case and although the food served was as good as any they'd had since arriving in Spain she had little appetite. She and Ellie were obliged to share a large feather bed so she contained her misery and didn't allow a single tear to fall.

A sennight later they were back at the port. John had no difficulty reselling the carriage and horses and was able to book them passage on the very same small ship they'd travelled over in. She remained outwardly calm, happy to be returning to civilisation once more, and pushed her grief deep inside.

Once back in England John immediately booked a cabin on a packet that would convey them all to the seaside town of Margate which, she had been reliably informed, was a delightful place to spend the summer weeks.

She'd written a letter to her grace saying that her engagement to Patrick was over and that she was spending the summer in Margate and would return, if that was convenient, in October. She promised to send her new address as soon as she was settled.

★ ★ ★

Margate was a delightful little seaside town and the bracing air would no doubt restore her appetite and spirits. They were obliged to stay at a hotel for a few days until John was able to rent them a small house in Hawley Square. This was adjacent to Cecil Square which was far more prestigious and way above her budget.

The house faced the pretty central garden and was of recent construction. It had three spacious bedrooms and a box room, an attic for the servants, two reception rooms and an excellent kitchen. It came fully staffed with a cook-housekeeper, a bootboy and a maid of all work.

'John, you will take one of the larger chambers, Ellie you will have the box room and I'll have the one that faces the garden.'

'I think you might be wise to employ

an older woman as a companion, Miss Westley, and stop tongues from wagging.'

'As I don't intend to socialise at all whilst I'm here, I hardly think it matters. If I was attending functions and dances at the assembly rooms, then I agree with you. I'll do very well with just you and Ellie for company.

'If it's possible to hire two horses then I should like to explore the countryside with you. Will our funds run to that?'

'There's a livery yard we passed not more than half a mile from here. I'll investigate tomorrow. The leaflet you picked up on board says there are two circulating libraries as well as the sea bathing.'

'I shall certainly avail myself of the former but have no intention of investigating the latter. If I could swim that would be something I might enjoy but as I can't, I'll remain firmly on dry land.'

★ ★ ★

As she'd taken so little with her on her foreign travels she would be obliged to purchase material and make herself more underpinnings and two more gowns. She was an excellent seamstress, as was Ellie, and between them they should be able to sew what they needed. Her first task was to find a suitable emporium to purchase what she needed.

So the days passed pleasantly enough, having garments to make filled the time as did exploring Margate, and visiting the library. Her daily rides with John were also most enjoyable. She had intended to correspond with her friend but somehow never got around to sending her the address of the house she was living in.

Pretending that she was happy, pushing Patrick to the back of her mind, made things easier. She had been settled in Hawley Square for over a week when she had an unexpected visitor. Ellie not only left the drawing room door open but also pointedly took a seat in the corner so she could act as chaperone.

'Doctor Peterson, how extraordinary

to see you here. How did you discover my direction? Please, take a seat and explain yourself.'

'Her grace mentioned that you were now living in Margate and I've friends here so I took the opportunity to visit. It's a small town and I was soon able to locate you. I hope you don't mind me calling unannounced.'

Hannah was pleased that she'd got on one of her new gowns and was looking her best. She was thinner than she'd been before as her appetite hadn't returned but her hair had its lustre back and her face was still attractively tanned from her brief sojourn in Spain. Members of the *ton* would no doubt be horrified to see her complexion so changed but she thought being white was less attractive.

'I'm delighted to see you, sir, you can tell me all the news from home.'

13

Amanda was waiting for Richard to depart for the London docks with his prisoner before setting in motion their move back to the Dower House. He had told her he would be gone for five nights at least which gave her ample time to arrange everything.

The first thing was to get the new house cleaned from top to bottom and for Patrick's belongings to be removed from his accommodation and stored carefully in the attic. When she'd informed the staff that they were returning the news had been received with enthusiasm. There would be sufficient servants left behind to keep Radley Manor functioning normally so that when Mama and the bridal couple returned there would be no problems.

Of course, there would be the necessity to employ extra staff to replace those she was taking with her but that would be Sarah's task when she returned. There were always those in the locality eager to work for the family.

Richard's valet packed up his master's belongings ready for the move. From his expression he wasn't entirely confident he was doing the right thing. She did her best to reassure him although there was no necessity to do so.

'His grace didn't wish to be involved in the move. The new house is no longer creating dust and debris as the exterior walls are completed and the roof is now watertight. He has expressed a desire to be able to keep a closer eye on the interior and living half a mile away will be an advantage for all of us.'

'I understand, your grace, I'm just puzzled that his grace didn't mention it to me before he left.'

'Just ensure that everything in his closet and cabinets is packed carefully and ready to be moved tomorrow.'

Her things were soon in trunks as were all the other items in her bedchamber and sitting room. Beth ran in equally excited by this proposed transfer.

'Amanda, Miss Parsons has never been to the Dower House. I think she'll like it better there. What about Mama — will she come too?'

'Mama is away until the autumn as are Sarah and Paul and Miss Westley. Remember, sweetheart, that I told you that Sarah, Paul and Mama will remain here. It's only ourselves and Miss Westley who will be living in the Dower House.'

'Why isn't Cousin Richard here to help? Has he gone to Bath to see Mama?'

'No, Beth, he's gone to London on business.'

Miss Parsons appeared, calm and unflustered as usual despite the fact that her charge had escaped from her. 'There you are, Beth, we need you upstairs to help with your own packing. You don't want your precious dolls to be put in a box any old how, now do you?'

'I don't. They might be broken. I'm coming right away.'

★ ★ ★

It took Amanda all of the five days she had at her disposal to complete the move. She looked around with pleasure at what she'd achieved in so short a space of time. She loved this house, she was more comfortable here than she'd been at Radley Manor.

This edifice was considerably smaller than the Manor but quite big enough for them. There were six spacious bedrooms for the family all of which had both a dressing and sitting room. There were also three smaller bedchambers for visitors, plus an excellent nursery floor where Beth and her entourage would reside.

On the ground floor were adequate reception rooms and an excellent kitchen. The real advantage of being here was that the vegetable garden, and the dairy and poultry were now so close. These had always provided sufficient for the Sinclair family and the surplus was given to the villagers and tenants. This would make things easier as fresh produce wouldn't have to be transported every day to the kitchens of Radley Manor.

They would also have access to the far more extensive grounds, the large stables and the boating lake. The only disadvantage was the lack of a maze which Beth was inordinately fond of.

Richard had said he hoped to be back in five days but hadn't made any firm promises. It had been essential to have things established here before his return so he was presented with a *fait accompli* and would have to accept the changes.

He would be furious, would roar and shout at her, but he would come around eventually to her way of thinking and appreciate what she'd done and why she'd done it. Her eyes filled. She was a constant watering pot at present and brushed away the moisture with her sleeve. She really didn't like being at odds with him and feared that it might take more than her apology to smooth things over.

Her appetite had deserted her these past few days and she hoped now that she'd accomplished her goal, she'd begin to feel more herself. She walked around the house running her fingers over the furniture, tweaking the occasional garden bloom in a vase, and was satisfied everything looked as it should.

Beth was delighted to be back and was happily playing with her dolls upstairs before having nursery tea. There'd been no dinner cooked today, but supper would be served later as Richard was expected to be here by then.

She walked to the stables to check that her beloved stallion, Othello, and the other horses were grazing peacefully in one of the meadows that ran parallel to the numerous outbuildings. These had been built for the family when they had lived in the ancient building which had been demolished to make way for the new.

There'd been no necessity to rebuild these coach houses, barns and stables as they were perfectly adequate. Having spoken to the horses she continued on her walk to the family chapel where she and Richard had been married a few months ago. The door was always open during the day and she went inside to commune with the Almighty.

It was cool and peaceful inside. Someone had placed fresh flowers on the altar and the rows of wooden chairs were polished, the flagstone floor swept clean. She walked to the side of the chapel then sat and bowed her head in reverence. It had been a tiring few days and not only had she not eaten well but had also not had much sleep without Richard at her side.

She closed her eyes and let her thoughts drift. From a distance she could hear the sounds of the countryside and she smiled and fell asleep.

★ ★ ★

Patrick pushed all thoughts of what might have been aside and concentrated on his duty. He was taciturn and no longer friendly with the men or the officers, but nobody commented. There'd been no need to explain what had transpired as it was patently obvious his engagement had been terminated.

The three companies marched more briskly, the officers behaved as they should and a week after his disastrous meeting with Hannah he found Wellington and his army.

The town of Ciudad Rodrigo had high walls and an old castle that dominated the surrounding countryside. One might have thought that being built like this it would be impregnable but the artillery were making headway with the heavy guns. They had been able to hear them pounding from miles away.

He rode up and down the column reassuring the soldiers that were staring apprehensively ahead. 'You won't be needed to fight for a while, not until there are breaches in the wall. The easy life for you boys until that's done.'

He was obliged to admit that this was a most attractive small town. The Agueda River ran around the town before heading northwards towards the sea. The

Moors had built the original battlements that surrounded it and a lot of these were still evident. It was going to be a hard place to breach.

This place wasn't far from the Spanish-Portuguese border which made it a crucial fort to hold for either side. Wellington's army had already surrounded the fortress. There would be brigades deployed to cover any attack from a French division coming to relieve Marshal Ney. There was the constant noise of the sappers digging the trenches along which both men and guns would be taken. These men worked in shifts both night and day.

He could no longer be in command, it was the duty of the officers, however mediocre they were, to present themselves to someone more senior and then discover to which division they were being attached. His task was to have the men stand at ease and await their orders.

He didn't officially belong to these companies and had no idea where General Boyden, the man who'd made his life so difficult this past year, might be stationed — if he was here at all. The general had been determined to get him to re-enlist and had gone to extravagant lengths to find him. Hopefully, arriving under his own volition would give him the advantage.

Patrick abandoned his temporary command and went in search of Wellington. Although obviously not an officer from his uniform, the fact that he was riding such a magnificent horse gave him access to areas not usually available to sergeants of any description.

He was scanning the tents, looking for a cluster of marquees that would indicate the supreme commander's whereabouts. He stood in his stirrups and saw at once the direction he should go. He was approaching what he took to be Wellington's headquarters when someone hailed him.

'Patrick, what the devil are you doing here? I thought you and Richard was lazing about as civilians somewhere in the English countryside.' Major Hogan, a good friend of Richard's, strode over to stand by his stirrup.

'I need to see Wellington, is he here or on patrol?' He dismounted and shook the major's hand. 'More importantly is that bastard Boyden here? He's been trying to have me arrested as a deserter.'

Hogan shook his head. 'Boyden perished some weeks ago. Not in battle — the silly bugger broke his neck falling off his horse when drunk.'

'I wish I'd known. I've had a wasted journey. No wonder there was no answer to the letters sent to Horse Guards and out here.'

Hogan snapped his fingers and a willing corporal approached and offered to take the reins. Bruno could join the other horses where he would be looked after better than the common soldiers. Patrick quickly removed his saddlebags and other belongings before handing his horse over.

'My tent's over there. Come with me, my friend. Do you have civilian clothes with you?'

'I do. I travelled this way to make it easier. I brought three companies down from Corunna and you'll be pleased to know that they're now in far better shape than they would have been without my involvement.'

Whilst he was hastily removing his uniform and replacing it with his somewhat crumpled other things he explained what had been happening with regards to his relationship with Boyden.

'The man's an idiot — I should say, was an idiot. I suppose you should be flattered that he thought that having you at his side would make such a difference. There's no need for you to speak to Wellington. I'd advise that you spend the night here, then collect your horse and head straight back to Corunna.'

'I was actually considering signing on again as I've enjoyed these past few weeks.'

'Don't be daft, man, make good your escape. It's damn boring work at the moment and when we attack in a few months time it will be a miracle if there's not a bloodbath. Go home, my friend, enjoy your good fortune.'

Over a decent bottle of wine, he found himself telling the major about Hannah.

'You obviously love the girl, go back to her, you imbecile, and be glad that you've got this opportunity to live out your life in comfort.'

'Good advice, Major, and I'll do exactly that if she'll still have me.' He hesitated and then told him about the final obstacle to his happiness.

'I can see that might be a sticking point, but if the girl loves you then she'll take you without children rather than marry someone she doesn't love in order to have some. However, I don't fancy your chances if you remain here much longer. This other blighter won't hang about, you know.'

* * *

Patrick set out at dawn the following day having sold his uniform easily. It was immediately snatched up by a sergeant

249

whose own wasn't in as good a condition. He kept his sword and pistol as they might come in useful during his long ride.

All went well until Bruno became lame after casting a shoe. He led his horse to a small village but there was no farrier here. He managed to make his needs known and someone was sent to fetch a blacksmith from the nearest town as he couldn't take the horse to him.

He'd picked up a smattering of Spanish over the past weeks and the family who'd taken him in were happy to instruct him in their language whilst he waited. Three days after his arrival he began to feel unwell and succumbed to a virulent fever.

The woman of the house took good care of him, he was vaguely aware of being sponged down, of having liquid trickled into his mouth, of his bodily needs being met, but had no notion of night or day or of how long he'd been abed.

When he was strong enough to sit up he was horrified to find that he'd been incapacitated for two weeks. The woman told him it would be another two weeks before he was strong enough to resume his journey. The only positive in all this was that Bruno was now fully recovered and his missing shoe replaced. All he had to do was regain his strength and pray that nothing else untoward delayed his return.

★ ★ ★

Hannah had been cloistered for so long without company that the unexpected arrival of the doctor made her livelier and more receptive to his conversation than might otherwise have been the case.

'Miss Westley, are you considering a return to Radley Manor at the end of the summer?'

'I am, sir, I thought to give her grace and his grace time alone as everyone else had gone away. My intention is to be back at the end of October.'

'I was surprised to hear that Mr O'Riley has gone to Spain. I thought he was settled as a civilian and looking to make his life here as his grace's man of business.' He paused and then continued. 'I'd heard that you and he were now betrothed.'

She wasn't entirely comfortable talking about Patrick but decided this might be a good opportunity to set the record straight. 'That's correct. He will be gone until the autumn so he suggested that I might like a change of scene as well until he returned.' Why hadn't she revealed that her betrothal had been broken and that the man she still loved had chosen the army over her?

'I see. I beg your pardon for intruding, Miss Westley. Forgive me, I've enjoyed our brief time together but must depart as I have another engagement.'

She scarcely had time to stand up before he bowed and disappeared as if his coat-tails were on fire. She was staring at the space he'd been occupying a few seconds before when Ellie spoke from behind her.

'He'd come to make you an offer, miss.

Why didn't you tell him the truth?'

'I don't know. I opened my mouth to say that my engagement to Patrick was over and said something else entirely. I only realised in that moment that I don't care about anything else but him. Please find John for me, I need him to book us a passage on the packet for tomorrow.'

When the young man appeared, instead of being encouraging as she'd expected, he shook his head. 'Forgive me for saying so, miss, but rushing back won't bring Mr O'Riley to your side. If he's made up his mind to stay where he is then it's too late.'

A heavy weight settled somewhere in her middle regions. 'Then you must go and find him. You know where he is; I'll write a letter at once and you can take it. I know I'm too late to stop him signing up but I want him to know that I'll wait for him, that I love him, that I'll marry him whatever his circumstances. No one else will do. I didn't understand that until Doctor Peterson came.'

Revealing her innermost thoughts to

a servant, even someone she knew and trusted as much as she did John, was unheard of. But the three of them had shared a great deal this summer and she would always think of them as friends as well as employees. She would never be so comfortable being an intimate of a duke and duchess. She was better seeking companionship amongst those of her own class, like Patrick, John and Ellie.

Now he was more enthusiastic. 'You get your letter written, miss, and I'll get my things packed. It might well take me a while to find him — but I give you my word he'll get your letter in person and I'll return with his reply.'

'My tenure in this house expires at the end of October. I'll remain here until then. That gives you seven weeks to complete your mission. I'll be residing at Radley Manor after that so come there to find me.'

This whole debacle could have been avoided if she'd not been so contrary. Her only excuse for vacillating from one position to another was that she didn't deal well with excitement, with change, and by behaving so out of character on that one night she'd thrown her composure and common sense into disarray.

For the remainder of her stay in Margate she took her walks early in the morning when there was no one else around. She felt vulnerable having no male servant to accompany her and was counting the days until she could resume her position as unpaid companion to the duchess. This was essentially what she'd become and she'd much prefer to be self-sufficient.

Patrick must have felt the same when he'd rejoined the army. He'd become his own man again, no longer dependent on the generosity of his former comrade-in-arms. Things fell into place and finally she understood his motivation. When he eventually returned he'd have sufficient money for them to buy themselves a small property somewhere. She could teach the daughters of well-to-do families, or perhaps they could set up a school together, but one thing she was quite sure of, was that she didn't wish to be reliant on the duke's benevolence.

14

The cold woke Amanda. For a moment she was disorientated, not sure where she was. Why was it dark in the chapel when sunlight was still filtering through the windows above the altar?

She shivered. Late October was warm enough during the day but decidedly chilly at night. She got up and moved into the central aisle and immediately understood why it was darker than it should be inside. Someone had closed the door.

She dashed to it and tried the latch but it was locked. The chapel was only closed at night — surely it couldn't be considered that time already? The sun set around eight o'clock so it couldn't be as late as that. There was little point in shouting as the chapel was too far away from the house for anyone to hear and it was also highly unlikely there would be labourers and other workers returning home this way.

One thing she could do that would help when eventually a search party was sent out to look for her was light all the candles in the chapel knowing that the light would reflect through the windows and could be seen from some distance away.

This activity kept her busy long enough for her to feel a little warmer. She was glad she'd got a warm wrap with her as it kept some of the autumn chill at bay. The chapel seemed less intimidating with so many candles burning. Her stomach gurgled loudly and she smiled. She hadn't eaten since last night so was now sharp-set and the thought of the delicious supper she'd planned for herself and Richard on his return made her mouth water.

If he was back he'd soon find her. She recalled last year when she'd been so distressed by events in London that she'd failed to sleep and had then done so on the ground in the woods. He had found her then and carried her back.

Even if she stood on a chair she would still be unable to see through the high windows but was confident the flickering golden light she'd created would be clearly visible after the sun set. There was a Bible on the lectern and after collecting it she settled down to read.

There was something that puzzled her and that was why she'd fallen asleep so readily in here and yet had been unable to do so in her comfortable bed? Her conclusion was that even after so short a time she needed Richard at her side.

The shadows lengthened, the chapel became colder, she began to think that no one had even noticed her disappearance. For some reason her beloved husband hadn't returned tonight as expected or he would already have come for her.

Jumping up and down and flapping her arms around made her a little warmer but her flimsy muslin gown was scant protection against the seeping cold. She was decidedly miserable, resigned to spending the night where she was, when she heard Richard approaching at the double. He was yelling her name and disturbing all the wildlife by doing so.

She was on her feet, laughing at his noise. 'I'm here, someone locked me in. The curate has the key.'

'I have an axe which will do just as well. Stand away from the door, sweetheart, I'm coming in.'

Hastily she backed away and then the door shook from a massive blow. Two further attacks and the ancient wood splintered and he was through.

'Idiot girl, what were you thinking to come here without telling anyone?' He had his jacket off and draped it, still warm from his body, around her shoulders. 'I would have been here earlier but wasted valuable time going to Radley Manor.'

'I'm sorry, I wanted the move to be a surprise.'

Two grooms had kicked the rest of the door to splinters whilst they were talking. 'Well, my darling, you succeeded there. Up you come, I'll carry you back.'

'I'm quite capable of walking, dearest Richard.'

His arms tightened and he kissed her fiercely. 'I know you are, but I need to have you safe in my arms just now.'

She looped her hand around his neck and argued no more. He covered the half a mile swiftly and bounded up the stairs and into their apartment.

'There's a bath waiting for you. A cold collation has been set out on the sideboard. I told them to bring two jugs of coffee on our return.'

There was no sign of her maid or his valet. An involuntary shiver ran through her and this time it had nothing to do with the temperature.

The bath had been installed quite recently and had one of the miraculous apertures in the base so all the dirty water could run away. More importantly it was large enough to accommodate both of them.

A considerable time later they emerged and she viewed the wreckage of the room with some dismay. 'Making love in there wasn't a sensible thing to do, my dear, I fear the ceiling might collapse below from all the water we spilt.'

Unabashed he snatched up a large towel and enveloped her in it. 'I forgive you for transporting us here without discussing it first for the bathroom alone. Stand still whilst I dry you.'

She wriggled away from him laughing. 'I'm quite capable of doing that for myself, sir, I suggest you take care of your own needs. Parading around as you are is not respectable for a man in your position.'

His smile was wicked. 'The last thing I intend to be tonight, darling, is respectable.'

'There will be no more nonsense until I've eaten. For the first time in weeks my appetite's returned. We shall talk whilst we eat like sensible people.'

They cleared the delicious supper that had been left for them and drank both pots of coffee. Over the meal she told him why she'd wanted to return to the Dower House.

'Radley Manor belongs to Sarah and Paul now and it makes sense for Mama to remain there so Paul's mother is under the same roof as him. I didn't feel comfortable there and am happy to be home again.'

He slowly put down his cutlery, wiped his mouth on the napkin, and turned his chair so he was facing her. There was an expression on his face that she didn't recognise. Her heart began to beat faster. Was he really angry with her or was she worrying unnecessarily?

'That's not what's been making you unhappy, my love. I worked it out, eventually, for myself. You're disappointed that there's no sign of a baby as yet.'

'What use am I to you if I can't provide you with an heir?'

'I married you because I couldn't live without you, because you changed my life, because I love you to distraction. I don't give a damn whether we have a quiver full of daughters and no sons or the reverse. I do want children with you, but that's not the reason I married you.

'I'd be content with none if I didn't know how miserable you would be without little ones around your feet.'

He reached out and brushed away her tears with his thumbs. 'We've been married three months . . .'

'We must let nature take its course, sweetheart, I'm certain we'll have a family eventually. To be honest, I'm relieved rather than the reverse that so far you're not increasing. I don't want you to produce a baby every year and the amount of time we spend . . .'

'There's no need to go into detail, Richard. I hadn't thought of it like that. Mama only had the three of us and even though she no longer shared a bed with Papa after Beth was born, there could have been half a dozen children in the intervening years.'

Imagining her parents doing what she and Richard did made her feel decidedly uneasy. In fact the whole conversation wasn't to her liking. She changed the subject.

'Do you think that Patrick has really re-enlisted?'

'It's possible, but would be contrary to

everything he said to me. That reminds me, if he does come back he too will be somewhat surprised to find he's been evicted.'

'He can hardly live here if Hannah is doing so after they've terminated their engagement. That reminds me, you have a pile of correspondence to deal with. I put it on the bureau by the window.'

He strolled across and the silk bedrobe, which was all he had on, clung to his shoulders emphasising their breadth and musculature. She was naked beneath her robe and despite having eaten enough to feed a small army the thought of tumbling back into bed with him made her tingle all over with anticipation.

'God's teeth! That damned general, the one who caused all the trouble for Patrick, is dead. Horse Guards have decided not to pursue the matter and he's no longer considered a deserter.'

★ ★ ★

Patrick set out for Corunna exactly a month after he'd fallen ill with the ague. He'd paid the family well for looking after him but was now eager to get back to England and try to convince Hannah that marriage to him without children would be better than no marriage at all.

He'd come to the conclusion during his convalescence that she'd not make any hasty decisions. She wouldn't move on, pretend she didn't love him, as he'd initially feared and become betrothed to the quack. He was weak as a kitten, scarcely able to sit straight in the saddle. Bruno sensed this and plodded ahead refusing to do more than jog even when asked to do so.

The Señora had said it would be weeks before he was fully recovered and that he should take things easy until then. His life had been saved by the administration of a tisane made from something called Jew's bark. He'd heard about this in India but had never suffered from the ague so had taken little notice of its miraculous properties.

God knows where that poor family had obtained some, but he'd paid them handsomely and she'd given him a small pouch with the bark in it in case he suffered from this again. He recalled some poor fellow who'd died from it and sincerely hoped this was his last brush with mortality for a while.

Being killed in battle was something a soldier expected — but to die from a fever was a different thing entirely.

Somehow he remained upright and able to point Bruno in the correct direction but it took him twice as long to return to the port as it should have done. He wasn't entirely sure of the date, but thought it to be the middle of October by now judging by the weather.

This time he couldn't stay in the same inn as he was no longer a military man. He wasn't entirely sure where he should go. The way he was feeling it was quite likely he'd be robbed, if not worse, by one of the nasty looking coves that hung about the port looking for easy pickings.

He had his pistol but doubted if confronted he'd have time to prime, load and fire it. There were definitely two rough looking villains shadowing him. Like vultures circling a dying animal they sensed that he was vulnerable.

He straightened his shoulders, deliberately pulled out his weapon and made it ready to fire. He then glared across at the men hoping to attack him and pointed his gun at the nearest. His other hand rested on the hilt of his sword making it abundantly clear he could deal with both of them before they could do him harm.

They slunk away but he was certain they'd be back if he didn't find himself somewhere secure for the night. He didn't want Bruno stolen either. He tensed as a man called out to him to stop. Was this voice known to him?

'Mr O'Riley, I can't believe my good fortune to find you here and thus save my having to travel to Cuidad Rodrigo in search of you.'

John arrived at his side but his happy smile faded to one of concern. 'My, sir, you don't look too clever. Here, lean on me and I'll help you dismount. Give me your pistol. Don't want it going off half-cocked, do we now?'

His valet was talking to him as if he was a child unable to make decisions for himself. He was too unwell to remonstrate. He remembered little after that until he woke up with John sitting beside him.

'How long have I been out?'

'A week, sir, so I've sent for reinforcements. You're in a bad way and I doubt I'll get you home without assistance.' He pointed to a jug standing on small wooden table by the bed. 'I boiled up some of that bark and it worked a treat.'

Patrick's head began to clear. 'Reinforcements? Who?'

'I wrote to his grace and two stout coves turned up this morning. One's taken Bruno out for some exercise and the other's sorting out the laundry and such. I reckon between the three of us we can get you safely back.'

The way he felt at the moment he seriously doubted he'd ever get out of bed again. Having never been ill in his life before he had no faith in his ability to get over this. A bayonet in the arm, a sabre slash on the thigh — he'd recovered from those in no time.

'Why are you here? Who sent you?'

'Miss Westley did. I've a letter for you.'

Patrick broke the seal and read the contents. She loved him still. She wanted to wait for him and would marry him as soon as he returned. He closed his eyes knowing in that moment he would recover as he now had something to live for.

The men Richard had sent were not from Denchester but hired in London. They hauled him out of bed regardless of his wishes and half-dragged, half-marched him around the room twice a day. He was plied with soup initially, then solid food and given watered wine to drink.

The rough treatment had angered him initially but within a few days he was more or less upright and able to leave for England. His clothes hung on him and for the first time in his life he allowed someone else to shave him.

John shared a small cabin with him and took care of his needs like a mother hen. He slept through most of the journey just waking to relieve himself and eat. When they docked he was considerably better and able to walk down the gangplank without aid. He wasn't so sure about his ability to ride the fifty miles to Denchester. They parted company with the extra men as he no longer needed their assistance.

'We'll stop here tonight, then I'll hire a carriage . . . '

'I've a better idea, John. I'll travel by stagecoach and you can ride Bruno. We'll overnight at the Saracen's in Chelmsford and again at the Red Lion in Colchester.'

'That's all very well, sir, how are we going to get from Ipswich to Denchester with only one horse?'

'It's only five miles. I'll ride and you can walk.'

'Fair enough. You look a deal better than you did two weeks ago but I'm not sure you're up to riding even five miles. And another thing, sir, you won't want to see Miss Westley looking like you do. We'll go straight to the Dower House and not tell her you're back until you don't look like you're going to kick the bucket at any moment.'

'Does she know how ill I've been?'

'Only his grace knows that. I didn't write to her. Better that you tell her when you're on your feet.'

* * *

Hannah decided it would be less stressful travelling by stagecoach from Margate to London as she was without a male attendant. There was too much opportunity for her to be waylaid by an opportunist whilst aboard the sailing packet.

A letter to her grace had been posted yesterday so would arrive several days before she did. There would be no smart carriage to convey her back this time but she was confident she and Ellie would manage both journeys without problems.

It was with considerable relief that she finally disembarked in Ipswich five days later. Ellie went in search of the landlord and was able to hire a small carriage and driver to convey them the last five miles. It would be late by the time they arrived at Radley Manor but as they were expected that should be no difficulty.

The door was opened by a footman she didn't recognise. He stared at her as if she wasn't anticipated.

'I am Miss Westley. This is my home and I am back from Margate. Stand aside and let me in at once.'

The man looked bemused but did as she asked. There were voices coming from the drawing room and she recognised one of them as Sarah's.

'Take my trunk to my chamber.' She smiled encouragingly at Ellie, waiting for her to take her travelling cloak, bonnet, gloves and reticule. 'Do I look respectable enough to go in as I am or should I leave it until tomorrow?'

'I'd leave it until tomorrow, miss. They'll be going up any time and not expecting visitors.'

She looked around but the footman and her trunk had vanished. Good — she could retire and greet her friends when she was rested and dressed in something clean.

The bed was freshly made, there was water in the jug in the dressing room. Ellie lit a candle from a wall sconce outside the bedchamber and then lit the others in the room. She was completing her ablutions and waiting for Ellie to appear with her nightgown.

'There ain't anything here, miss, none of your things in the closet. No sign of your trunk neither.'

'I'm too tired to worry about that now. I'll sleep in my petticoats and you must do the same. Everything can be sorted out tomorrow. I expect our things have been moved to another bedchamber for some reason.'

'It's ever so strange, miss, her grace knew you were coming.'

'She did indeed, it's a mystery but not one I wish to solve tonight. It's good to be back after so long and with any luck John will return with a letter from Mr O'Riley in the next week or two.'

15

Hannah slept fitfully and was up before Ellie appeared with the necessary hot water. She was mystified by her grace's actions as hadn't she already been moved from her chamber on the nursery floor to this one not so long ago?

There could be only one explanation. After discovering that someone she considered to be a close friend had behaved so immorally she had moved Hannah's belongings back to the nursery floor or possibly the servants' quarters.

Hastily she pulled on yesterday's gown, arranged her hair and decided to investigate for herself. Better that she removed herself to her new abode without embarrassing her grace. She had no choice but to remain here, however difficult it was, until Patrick replied.

She slipped out through her door. There was the faint sound of maids scrubbing the floors downstairs but not a whisper from any of the family chambers. There had been a pretty clock in the room but that too had gone so she'd no notion of the exact time, but thought it must be around five in the morning.

She must be careful not to wake Beth or her new governess. She halted midway up the flight of stairs. She wasn't thinking clearly. Her grace could hardly put her on the nursery floor as someone else was occupying that space. She reversed her steps uncertain what to do next.

There was no option but to return to this bedchamber until the family were up and then confront the problem head-on. From this point forward things were back the way they should be as far as she was concerned. There would be no further use of given names. She'd never been comfortable with the idea of addressing his grace as Richard so had not referred to him at all by name.

Lady Sarah was definitely home from her wedding trip as she'd heard her talking to someone last night. Presumably the dowager duchess was also back from

Bath with Mrs Marchand and the house would once more be full. Without Patrick she was lost, had no place in this family or any other. If he rejected her offer then she would seek employment knowing that she would get a glowing reference whatever the circumstances of her leaving.

Ellie burst in an hour later. 'We've come to the wrong house, miss, her grace went back to the Dower House two weeks ago. They will be expecting us there.'

'Then who is living here?'

'Lady Sarah and Mr Marchand, also her grace and Mrs Marchand. Your trunk's here now so you can change your gown and I've pressed everything in it. Someone will have told Lady Sarah so we can't creep off again.' Ellie wasn't usually so talkative but this extraordinary turn of events had loosened her tongue.

'At least I can meet her looking smart. I'm sure they'll let us use a carriage to transfer but it won't be until after breakfast I expect.' Dressed in one of her new gowns, her hair now dressed in a more becoming style, she was ready to descend and apologise for her unexpected arrival last night.

* * *

Amanda was at the breakfast table with Richard when a footman came in with a note from Sarah. Puzzled at this early arrival of correspondence she opened it and perused the contents.

'Good gracious me! I neglected to inform Hannah that we'd moved and she went to Radley Manor.'

'As she failed to give us her address in Margate then you could hardly have done so, my dear. It must have come as somewhat of a surprise for your sister to have Hannah arriving on her doorstep.'

'That's what's so amusing, my love. Sarah didn't know until just now that she had a guest. A new footman let them in last night and Hannah retired immediately. She must have been so shocked to discover her belongings had vanished mysteriously from what she believed to be her room.'

'Dammit to hell! I've done precisely the same thing myself. When I arranged for . . . ' His voice trailed off and he swore again much to her annoyance.

'Do go on, Richard, what did you arrange? Please refrain from using such bad language when you explain yourself.'

'I got letter from John asking for my help. Patrick's very ill, he's been struck down with the ague and twice now has almost died. I didn't want to worry you.'

Her breakfast threatened to return and she swallowed hastily. 'I understand why you refrained from informing me, but you promised not to keep secrets from me anymore. I'm upset that Patrick's so unwell but far more upset at your perfidy. Excuse me, I no longer wish to share a table with you.'

He was on his feet and moving towards her before she was halfway to the door. He knew better than to physically restrain her but stood in her way quite pointedly.

'Please, Amanda, don't let us fall out

over this. My omission was done with the best of intentions.'

'I'm sure it was. However, I'm going to my apartment as I don't feel at all well. Kindly get out of my way.'

His eyes narrowed. His expression was glacial. 'I accepted your overstepping your position by transferring my house-hold here and this is how you repay my forbearance?'

'Feel free to move back to Radley Manor if you wish to, your grace, I am remaining here.' She waited staring straight ahead, not daring to meet his eyes, until he stepped aside.

She stalked through but instead of going upstairs she went outside. She would walk in the cool privacy of the woods until she calmed down. Presumably, Hannah and her maid would arrive sometime this morning and they would expect to speak to her. Therefore, she couldn't remain outside for more than an hour.

After wandering about breathing in the damp, fresh smell of the moss, the lush grass and the ferns that grew under the canopy of trees she was ready to return. She would be civil to Richard, she could hardly be anything else, but he wasn't forgiven for breaking his word yet again to always include her in his decisions.

Legally she was his property, had no rights at all, so how could she in all conscience complain when he behaved as any other husband? Was she wrong to rail at him for excluding her from his life? The painful conclusion to this question was that he had every right to behave as he wished and she had no recourse but to accept it.

Sadly she came to the unplatable realisation that in future things must be different between them. She would be a compliant wife, ask nothing from him, do her duty as she was brought up to do, but the joy had gone from her union.

If he wished to share her bed he must come to her in future, she would no longer sleep beside him every night. This was one area of their marriage that she could still enjoy although she wondered if he would continue to visit her if, as she feared, she was barren.

Hannah arrived but Richard didn't come out to greet her. The young woman who she now considered as a friend didn't rush to embrace her as she'd expected but curtsied as if to a stranger.

'I apologise for my error, your grace, if I'd written sooner then you could have replied and told me of the change in circumstances.' Amanda was about to remonstrate for this formality but Hannah continued. 'I hope you will allow me to remain here until I hear from Patrick. I wrote to him and sent John with the letter saying that I wish to marry him after all whatever the circumstances. I cannot be elsewhere until I hear from him, I hope this will be acceptable.'

'Hannah, what's wrong? I thought we were friends. The world has gone mad at the moment and I don't understand how things have come to this. Please, we need to talk somewhere we won't be disturbed.'

She gave her no option but to follow

and she led her to the small, sunny room at the rear of the property that was for her exclusive use.

'Sit down, my dear, I have news for you that will be most difficult for you to hear.'

Hannah's colour faded and she collapsed onto the nearest chair. 'Is he dead? Please don't tell me that he's been killed.'

'No, but he's very unwell. He caught the ague whilst with Wellington and John has been taking care of him. He should be back with us in a week or so. The general who wished to force him to re-enlist is dead, so he is now a civilian again.'

'Did he get my letter?'

'I'm sure he did. He cannot reply himself as he's been too ill to write but when John found him in Corunna he was on his way home. He could have re-enlisted if he so wished but obviously chose to come back to you instead.'

'Then I must pray that he gets here safely. Forgive me, your grace, but I'm not comfortable being on such familiar terms with you and his grace. When Patrick and I are reunited we'll find somewhere in the vicinity to live. Obviously, his employment is here so we can't move far.'

Amanda bit her lip. Today was turning into a disaster. First she'd fallen out with Richard and now someone she'd considered a bosom bow had reverted to the position of an employee rather than a friend.

'Do you wish me to revert to calling you Miss Westley?'

'I would prefer it if you would, your grace. It restores the natural order of things in my eyes. I am the daughter of a country vicar, my future husband's a common soldier who only became part of this circle by dint of being a comrade-in-arms of the duke for so long. We don't belong here. We must find our own way in the world.'

'I shall respect your wishes, my dear Miss Westley, but whatever you might think to the contrary I'll always consider you part of this family.'

Hannah stood up and curtsied making it quite clear that their intimacy was over. 'Forgive me, your grace, but would it be permissible for me to be shown my new accommodation? I would then like to speak to Lady Beth.'

Sadly she stood up and walked to the bell-strap and pulled it. 'You don't have to ask my permission to do anything, but thank you for doing so. My sister will be delighted to see you and has talked of little else these past few days. She insists that next summer we too must go to Margate or somewhere similar.'

A footman answered the bell and took her erstwhile friend away with him leaving her bereft.

★ ★ ★

Patrick thought the longer he took over his return the better it would be for his reunion with his love. He'd been shocked by his emaciated appearance and didn't wish to upset his future wife by looking like a walking corpse.

286

On their arrival in Ipswich he decided to remain at the posting inn for a further few days in order to continue to regain his strength and hopefully improve his appearance.

'John, I need to purchase both a wedding and a betrothal ring before I continue my journey. I'm not looking today I'm too fatigued but will, with your able assistance, go in search of these items tomorrow.'

'Do I write to his grace and tell him that we're remaining in Ipswich for a few days? I'm certain he'll send a vehicle of some sort to collect you and save me from the walk. The weather's turned and although I don't fancy getting drenched, it's more important that you don't get wet. If you catch a congestion of the lungs it'll see you off, that's for sure.'

He laughed at his friend — John was that now as well as his valet. 'Then by all means send a missive to the duke. Although, I think it might be better if I wrote myself. I wonder if Hannah has returned from Margate yet?'

'I reckon so, it's a mite blustery and cold by the sea this time of the year. I'll speak to the landlord and let him know to expect a visit from a duke. That'll get you a fine room for sure.'

'This one is perfectly adequate. I'm a rough soldier, albeit a remarkably feeble one at present, and I'm quite content where I am.' He smiled. 'But, don't let that stop you. I owe you my life, John, as far as I'm concerned you can do as you damn well please.'

'I'll sit over there and let you write your letter, sir, then will have it delivered immediately.'

Patrick started without preamble. He told Richard how unwell he'd been, thanked him for his help so far, and said that he was now recovering. He also asked if Hannah was there and if so to pass on his love. He paused and then added a few more words and signed it with a flourish.

After sanding the wet ink, he folded the page, melted the wax and pressed the borrowed seal into it. John went off whistling and he kicked off his boots and flopped out on the bed. Gone were the days when he had to ask for assistance to remove his footwear as now they were so loose they were bordering on uncomfortable.

He fell into a deep sleep, thought he heard voices in the room but they didn't disturb him so he returned to his slumber. When he eventually opened his eyes he saw Richard sprawled on the chair beside his bed watching him. His friend grinned.

'Thank God. For a while I thought I was watching a cadaver.' He offered his hand and Patrick took it.

'I can't tell you how glad I am to see you again. There was a time when I thought I'd see no one I knew before meeting my maker. I blame General Boyden for this. If I hadn't had to traipse all the way across Spain I'd never have caught this wretched illness.' He swung his feet to the floor, stood up and embraced Richard.

'You look as bad as I'd expected, but

289

I think you're past the worst. Hannah's with us but I didn't tell her you were here. In fact, I didn't tell anybody.'

'What's going on, my friend? Are you and Amanda at odds?'

This was the wrong thing to say as Richard's expression changed and he was no longer speaking to a friend but a formidable aristocrat.

'I beg your pardon, major, none of my damned business. I thought to stay here until I'm more recovered but, if you don't mind, now I know that Hannah's waiting for me . . .'

Richard smiled but it was a poor attempt. 'Don't worry, I've spoken to the vicar. You can be wed as soon as you return.' He then laughed. 'I forgot to tell you a pertinent fact. You've been turfed out of your home and I now live at the Dower House. Beth and her new governess came with us, and now Hannah is there too, but the others have remained at Radley Manor.'

'Then where the hell will Hannah and I reside? I thought we'd be there so I can continue as your man of business. I can't marry her until I've found somewhere for us to live.'

'Leave it to me. There must be somewhere in my demesne that will suit. I'll take Bruno and leave the gig here.' He turned to go and then pointed to the corner. 'I've brought you fresh garments although I doubt any of them will fit properly now.'

No sooner had the door closed behind the major than John knocked and came in. 'His grace drove himself. I've seen to the horse. There's food coming up for you and then hot water.'

* * *

Over the next few days Patrick continued to improve, he was eating enough for two and able to stay awake most of the day. He had managed to purchase both rings and was now ready to return as a letter had come that morning saying the major had found him a decent house with a couple of acres, a kitchen garden, and was both staffed and furnished. Not only that, both his and Hannah's belongings were being transferred to their new home immediately. There was no obstacle to their being married at once.

'John, you know the neighbourhood better than I. Where exactly is this Bagshot Hall?'

'It's on the edge of Denchester village, sir, no more than a mile or two from Denchester itself. Will I be coming with you?'

'You'd better. I'll not have any other looking after me.'

'Do you think that Ellie will accompany Miss Westley?'

'I'm certain she will. Are you interested in her?'

John grinned making him look like an eager schoolboy. 'We've a bit of an understanding already, sir, would you and Miss Westley have any objection if we make a match of it?'

'I certainly don't, but I can't speak for my future wife. Which reminds me, I'm hoping to be married immediately and would like you to be a witness.'

'I'd be honoured, sir, but forgive me for saying so, I reckon you might be wise to leave it another week or two.'

He knew exactly what John was hinting at. 'I can assure you the way I feel about my bride I'll be able to do my duty, never fear.'

Two hours later they were sitting side by side on the seat of the gig heading for the Dower House. He'd just scrambled out when his beloved erupted into the stable yard much to the amusement of the watching grooms.

He opened his arms and she thew herself into his embrace. She was where she was meant to be.

16

Hannah clung onto Patrick horrified at
the change in him since she'd seen him
last. He'd lost so much weight but his
arms were still as strong as ever.

Ignoring the grinning audience she
buried her fingers into the hair at the
back of his neck and pulled his face
down so they could kiss. He didn't need
further encouragement and by the time
he raised his head she was incandescent
with happiness.

'I'm so sorry, my love, you would never
have been so unwell if I'd not broken the
engagement.'

'It would have been more likely that
you would have caught it too. I'm back
now and I've something for you.' With
one arm firmly around her waist he
delved into his waistcoat pocket with his
free hand and pulled out a small leather
box. He flicked it open and inside was
the most unusual betrothal ring.

'Patrick, that's perfect. Wherever did you find such a thing? Is that gold and silver twisted together and then set with pearls?'

'It's from Ireland, sweetheart, I couldn't believe my luck when I discovered this. Here, let me put it on your finger then I'll know you're mine.'

She held out her hand and it slipped perfectly over the knuckle as if made for her. 'It's absolutely perfect. Shall we go in as I think we've made a sufficient spectacle of ourselves out here, don't you?'

'Not yet, I have two things that I need to tell you. I want to marry you today. The vicar's waiting for us to send him word.'

'Today? I don't know. I must tell you that things have changed here, for me at least. I don't really wish to start my married life with you under this roof but under one of our own. I no longer refer to his grace or her grace by anything but their titles.'

'You didn't let me tell you the second piece of news.'

She could hardly credit what he said. 'His grace is happy for us to live as his tenants in this house? I can't tell you how happy I am. When can I see it?'

He laughed and swung her around as if she was a child. 'We'll see it together for the first time when we are wed, sweetheart. Now, stop dithering about out here. I'm an invalid and need to regain my strength before we set off for the church.'

'And I need to change into something more suitable as a bridal gown.'

'I should have thought of that but I fear that you'll find that all your things will now be packed and are being taken to Bagshot Hall even as we speak.'

'Well I suppose it's of no account really. After all, I'm marrying a red-headed scarecrow in ill-fitting garments and it would never do for a wife to appear smarter than her husband.'

The duke and duchess were waiting to greet them inside looking decidedly pleased with themselves for having deceived her so royally.

'Beth is just putting on her bonnet, Sarah and Paul will be on their way to the church as a message was sent to them as soon as Patrick was seen approaching. All you have to do is put on your bonnet and pelisse, my dear, and we can depart as well.'

Patrick had vanished with the duke leaving her alone with her grace. 'I don't want any fuss, ma'am, I just want to marry him and take him to our new house so I can look after him and nurse him back to full health.' She swallowed a lump in her throat and blinked back tears. 'I'm shocked to see how thin he is. He was always a robust and healthy man. I've read about this dreadful illness and know that it can recur sometimes years later and is always dangerous.'

'I've spoken to Doctor Peterson and he's already sent for a supply of this precious bark so that you've got it to hand if such a thing occurs.'

They went upstairs together to find their bonnets and pelisses. Ellie was beside herself with excitement.

'Everything's packed and been taken downstairs. I was that fearful that you'd come back to your chamber and see what was going on. It was to be a surprise arranged for you by Mr O'Riley.'

Laid out on the bed was one of the gowns that she and Ellie had made in Margate that had yet to be worn. It was in warm chenille, a lovely damask pink, with long sleeves and matching spencer. She'd been puzzled by Ellie's insistence that she wore her red half-kid boots this morning but now she understood.

'Quickly, help me change. Thank you so much for your help. I'm so excited my hands are shaking.'

She was touched to see that her maid had added matching damask ribbons to her best bonnet so her ensemble was quite perfect.

'Ellie, you're to come with me. I wish you to see us married. John will, no doubt, accompany Patrick.'

Downstairs Beth was waiting in her best gown with Miss Parsons, and her grace had also changed into a fresh gown and looked every inch a duchess.

'Where is Patrick and his grace?'

'Good heavens, he could hardly wait here and see his bride before she arrives at the church. He has gone ahead with Richard as he should. Come along, my dear, our carriage awaits.'

Hannah sat with Beth and her grace on one side of the carriage and Ellie and Miss Parsons sat on the other.

'I've an admission to make to you, my dear. Richard and I could not let our dearest friends celebrate their nuptials without providing a small wedding breakfast. It's all arranged and we shall return here to drink a toast to you both and share a meal before you depart for your new home.'

'That's so kind of you both and much appreciated. I shan't allow Patrick to return to work until I'm quite sure he's fully recovered.'

Her grace laughed. 'My husband's managed without him and I am quite sure can do so for another few weeks. That said, he's very relieved that Paul's returned and has taken back the running of the estate.'

Hannah was unable to continue this conversation, there was a lump in her throat making it impossible to swallow let alone speak. Maybe she'd been premature in distancing herself from someone who she loved as dearly as a sister. Perhaps, once she was a respectable married woman, she could send out cards and have an *at home* and thus establish cordial relations again.

She reached across and squeezed her companion's hand. The pressure was returned and she knew things would be easier in future.

* * *

Amanda hoped that her happy smile was convincing when actually she was feeling rather out of sorts. She'd remained in her own bedchamber and Richard had remained in his. Apart from the five nights when he'd been delivering Carstairs to the docks they'd never slept apart.

300

The wind had definitely been taken from her sails by his choosing to do exactly what she'd intended him to do. He was civil to her, pleasant even, but there was no intimacy. The banter, the teasing, the sharing of thoughts had gone to be replaced by something she wasn't happy with.

It was inexplicable to her that she should object to things being exactly as she wished. She could only think this was because it was he who'd instigated this new relationship rather than herself. He'd said to her only a few nights ago when he'd rescued her from the chapel that she was his life, that he loved her to distraction, so how could he now be treating her this way?

He was as affectionate as ever when anyone else was present but reverted to the coolness and formality when they were alone. He seemed perfectly content with this new arrangement and that too was a puzzle. Their night-time activities had been instigated by him — as was only right — and sometimes more than once a night. How could he now be sanguine to be celibate?

The carriage halted smoothly outside the small church and to her surprise there was already a goodly number of villagers gathered outside. Whether it was to wish the happy couple well, or just to alleviate the boredom of their day, she'd no idea.

As was customary the vicar was waiting to lead Hannah down the aisle. Richard handed them down from the carriage. It was to be his role to take her friend to the altar.

'You look quite beautiful, my dear. I'll see you inside.'

Good heavens — Mama and Mrs Marchand had also attended. There was almost a congregation present. She hurried to her seat at the front of the church and sat down with Beth and Miss Parsons beside her.

The clothes that had been altered to fit Patrick's new shape fitted perfectly. He stood proud and straight, staring back down the aisle waiting for his bride to appear. He looked handsome. Red

302

hair and green eyes was typically Irish and had never held much appeal for her but she was forced to admit that she was coming to appreciate this colouring.

Beth was staring at John who was presumably Patrick's groomsman. Before she could prevent it her sister spoke loudly enough to be heard by everyone. 'Why is Mr O'Riley's valet standing up there with him?'

'Lady Beth, John is standing as my friend. And I'm honoured to have him beside me.'

The small organ, that had been installed by Richard when he'd inherited the title, began to play music suitable for a bride walking down the aisle.

The small congregation stood and Richard looking even more attractive than usual in his dark blue topcoat, grey silk waistcoat and snowy white stock, took Hannah to the altar without even glancing in her direction.

As this was the third time she'd heard the wedding service this year she could almost repeat the words in her head.

Richard had taken a seat on the other side of the aisle, not sat next to her. Then she realised she'd not left a space for him so he'd no alternative but to sit elsewhere.

Vows were exchanged, the ring was placed on Hannah's finger, and they were pronounced man and wife. They led the small procession from the church and were greeted by a round of applause from the locals gathered by the lychgate.

Patrick lifted Hannah onto the high seat of the gig and then jumped in beside her. Her husband would have to travel in the carriage with her unless he got a lift with Sarah and Paul. This was unlikely as Mama and Mrs Marchand were also travelling in that vehicle.

She stood with Sarah and Beth and waved the happy couple off. 'I hope they get back in time as there are black clouds gathering and I think it's going to rain heavily soon.'

'In which case, Amanda, the sooner we're away the better. Will you allow me to hand you in to our carriage?'

This, she assumed, was a rhetorical question so she didn't bother to answer. As was often the case nowadays she got it wrong.

'Your grace, I asked you a question.'

'I beg your pardon, sir, I was wool-gathering. Thank you for your kind offer but I'm perfectly capable of getting into a carriage without your assistance. Do you intend to travel with us?'

There was a dangerous glint in his eyes when he answered. 'I've no intention of running along behind, my dear, so you must suffer my company for the journey.'

The steps were down so she skipped up and took her place on the far side of the carriage. Beth and Miss Parsons followed and then Richard got in. The coachmen kicked up the steps and slammed the door.

Fortunately, Beth filled the silence with gay chatter about everything and nothing which meant that she and Richard didn't have to speak to each other or anyone else.

As soon as the door was open and the steps down she was out of the carriage like a scalded cat and hurried, trying not to look as if she was doing so, into the house in the hope that she wouldn't have to exchange words with Richard.

That there would be words exchanged, and not friendly ones either, was a certainty. However, he would refrain from giving her a severe set down until the wedding breakfast was done and their guests departed. He would never let his anger ruin his friend's happiness.

Somehow she got through the celebration without revealing how upset she was. The one thing that did surprise her was that the doctor appeared as happy about the nuptials as everyone else. Perhaps his feelings for Hannah hadn't been as strong as everyone had thought.

The meal was interminable and she ate almost none of it. At last she was able to stand up and indicate to the ladies it was time to withdraw and leave the gentlemen to their port.

'Amanda, will you play for us whilst

we wait? I miss hearing you perform so beautifully on the piano in the evenings,' Sarah said as they walked into the drawing room.

The piano had been the first and most important item of furniture to be transferred and it appeared not to have suffered from the experience.

'I should love to. Is there anything particular you would like to hear?' She addressed this question to all the ladies but no one had any particular favourites and were all happy to leave the choice to her.

No sooner had her fingers run across the keys than she forgot her anxiety and lost herself in the music. She'd decided on a piano concerto by Bach that she loved and could play without recourse to the music. As the final notes faded she was jerked back to the present by her audience clapping loudly. She quickly closed the lid determined that would be the only piece of music she would play tonight.

Hannah had made it quite clear she

wished to depart with Patrick as soon as possible. As neither of them had seen Bagshot Hall she didn't blame them. She stood up and was about to join the others when her eyes blurred, her head spun and she was falling.

Familiar arms caught her before she hit the floor. 'Darling girl, I've got you. I knew there was something wrong.'

She was beginning to recover her senses but knew there was no point in asking him to put her down. He strode from the room, upstairs and into her own bedchamber. He placed her tenderly on the bed and then stood back.

'Peterson, my wife's been unwell for weeks. I'll leave you to make your examination.'

The last thing she wanted was to be examined by any gentleman that wasn't her husband. Then Mrs Marchand was at her side.

'I'll stay with you, your grace. His grace asked me to do so. He's pacing up and down outside the door.'

The doctor approached her, fully

professional and her concerns about being touched by him evaporated. 'My first question, your grace, is how many monthly courses have you missed?'

'None at all. They have been much lighter than usual these past two months but have still arrived on time. I know what you're thinking that I could be increasing. I thought the same myself as I've been feeling unwell and my bosom is tender to the touch but knew this couldn't be the case.'

He smiled. 'I'm certain that you are increasing, your grace. If you allow me to give you a quick examination I can confirm it. Do you know the last time you had a normal course?'

'I can't remember exactly but I think it must be more than three months ago.'

He politely turned his back and she heard him washing his hands at the washstand whilst Mrs Marchand raised her skirts for her and then covered her limbs with the sheet. The doctor's touch was impersonal and gentle.

'I can confirm that you are three

months along. You can expect a happy event next April. I can assure you it's not uncommon for a woman to experience what you have. You can continue to do everything that you normally do. The symptoms you've been experiencing, fainting, lack of appetite will settle down as the months go by. I can assure you that the chances of a miscarriage are slim now that you've passed three months.

'I'd advise against riding, but apart from that I don't consider pregnancy as an illness but a natural state of things for a healthy young woman.' He smiled and stepped back. 'I'll leave you to give the good news to his grace. Congratulations, your grace.'

Hastily she rearranged her clothing and scrambled out of bed. She smiled her thanks at Mrs Marchand who waved and vanished through the sitting room door leaving Richard to charge in from the corridor.

'I'm so sorry, I've been a brute to you. I thought to play you at your own game until you came to me wanting to end this nonsense. If I'd known you were so unwell . . . What did the damn doctor say?'

'I'm not ill, my darling, we're expecting a baby next April. It seems my reprehensible behaviour, tendency to squabble and burst into tears is caused by my condition.'

He didn't shout with joy, just took her hands, his eyes clouded with worry. 'I don't understand how that can be — you've not missed a monthly course at all.'

She quickly told him what the doctor had told her and finally he smiled. 'These past few days have been the most miserable of my life. I know this is what you wanted, that thinking you might not have a child has been making you unhappy, but you do realise you must have conceived on our honeymoon?'

'I was speaking to Mrs Marchand earlier and she assured me that there are things that can be done to avoid a yearly pregnancy that don't mean we have to stop making love.'

His eyes darkened and he drew her close. 'Do you think those downstairs will miss us if we remain up here?'

She leaned in until every inch of her was touching him. His heat burnt through the thin material of her gown. 'I don't care if they do. However, I want to go downstairs and give everyone our good news. This will be a first grandchild for my mother. Also, dearest, it would hardly be polite to abandon the bride and groom so abruptly.'

'Absolutely not as far as you're concerned. I'll go down and explain why you can't return. I'll be back after our guests have departed.'

17

Patrick sat with Hannah watching the door, waiting for the doctor to appear or for Richard to come and tell them why Amanda had collapsed.

'His grace is coming in now, Patrick.' Hannah, like everyone else, jumped to their feet not out of respect but because she was eager to hear his news.

'You may relax, I've the best possible information. We're expecting a happy event next April. It was a shock to both of us as the usual indication was not there. The doctor has advised that Amanda rests for a few days but there's no danger of losing the baby.'

Patrick was the first to congratulate his friend, and then the ladies followed and finally Paul added his good wishes. Richard drew him to one side.

'I was abrupt with you when you enquired about my marriage. Amanda hasn't been herself these past few weeks and now I know why. I don't give a damn myself about having an heir so soon, but for some reason she believed I would reject her if we didn't have children.'

'I don't think I can give Hannah a child. I've certainly had sufficient opportunity over the years but I know that none of my liaisons resulted in progeny. I told her before we married.'

His friend looked at him as if he was speaking in tongues. 'Good God, why the hell did you do that? I cannot think of anything less suitable to tell one's future wife than that you've had dozens of affairs with other willing females.'

'Peterson was sniffing around. I wanted her to balance the possibility of being childless and married to the man she loved, against his potential offer. As you can see, she made the right decision.'

More champagne was fetched and as they were about to raise their glasses Paul interrupted. 'Forgive me for stealing your moment, Major, but Sarah and I are also anticipating a happy event next year.'

Her grace, rather than looking pleased, seemed decidedly put out by this second announcement. 'I am far too young to be a grandmother. I was congratulating myself on the fact that I wouldn't be under the same roof as the first one and now discover a second will arrive to disturb my peace.'

Mrs Marchand gently took her grace's arm. 'Come, your grace, too much excitement isn't good for your nerves. Shall we take a short turn around the garden whilst we wait for our carriage to be harnessed?'

Richard instead of looking annoyed at his mother-in-law's comment looked worried. He moved to her side immediately. 'My dear Aunt Ellen, you've done so well these past few weeks. I think Mrs Marchand is right and it would be best for you to avoid further excitement for a while.'

She looked confused and then upset. 'Did I say something I shouldn't? I'm so sorry if I offended anyone. I must leave at once. Will you walk in the garden with me, dear boy, in case I become more unwell?'

The three of them left through the French doors that led onto the terrace. The ladies didn't even stop to put on their bonnets.

'I think that we should also take our leave, sweetheart, I'm eager to see our new home and it will be dark in an hour or two.'

There was a flurry of goodbyes and in a short space of time he was sitting beside his wife in the gig driving the two miles to Denchester and then to discover Bagshot Hall.

'Goodness me, we've forgotten about Ellie and John. How are they to get to their new home?'

'They walked from the church as it's only a few hundred yards. They will have everything ready for us. I still can't quite credit that you agreed to marry me when you could have had someone so much better.'

'I love you, Patrick, and no one else would do. My head's still spinning at the speed with which my life has changed over these past months. I don't know if you realise this about me, but I prefer things to remain the same. I like order, calm and a peaceful environment in which to live.'

He chuckled. 'And yet you still married me. I've never known a family to attract so much excitement and disruption — if you wished for a quiet life then you've married the wrong man.'

'There's something I'd like to do before we get home. Could we not speak to Mr Carstairs and tell him about his son? He might well be frantic not knowing what's happened to him.'

'I should think it more likely he's relieved the bast . . . the villain's no longer here to plague him. Do you want me to tell him why he was shipped off to India?'

It was her turn to laugh. 'I should think I do. You can hardly inform him that his eldest was forced to become a sailor by the duke without giving him the reason.'

'Do you wish to come in with me or

will you stay with the gig?'

'I'm quite content to sit here and wait on your return. I don't think there should be a lady present when you explain what happened. See, the vicarage is just ahead.'

With some reluctance he pulled on the break, looped the reins around the pole and jumped down. This was hardly something he'd expected to be doing on his wedding day — but then nothing about his life was straightforward and he doubted it ever would be as long as he was associated with the Denchester family.

He knocked more loudly than he'd intended. The door was opened by a flustered maidservant who immediately stepped aside to allow him to go in.

'The master is in his study, sir, I'll conduct you to him immediately.'

Far too quickly he was standing in front of the reverend gentleman who'd not only just married him, but also joined Richard and Amanda and Paul and Sarah in holy matrimony.

'Forgive me for intruding, Mr Carstairs, but my wife insisted that I must tell you something that will cause you pain.' He explained the reason for his visit and the poor man flopped onto the nearest chair.

'I feared something far worse. I thought him dead. I wouldn't have blamed his grace in the circumstances if his decision had been less lenient. I don't know where we went wrong with that boy, he was always wild but that turned into viciousness.' He sighed loudly and shook his head.

'I'm sorry to have had to be the one to tell you this. His grace has made sure your son will have sufficient to buy his passage home. He'll only have to work going out to India.'

'I must apologise for what he attempted to do. The old duke insisted he would pay for him to have the best education available and I think it gave the boy ideas above his station. Do you wish me to inform my wife of the true state of affairs?'

'You must do as you think right, sir.

I can assure you that the few of us who know will never talk of it again. One thing I must ask you, do you think your son will blab when he returns?'

'He'll not come back here, I give you my word on that. Anything he says to the detriment of his grace and his family will be ignored. Thank you for telling me. I cannot like the boy, but I will always love him and will forgive him as the good Lord has instructed us to do when he is ready to ask to be forgiven.'

They shook hands and Patrick walked out glad that Hannah had insisted he did this. Now there was no obstacle in the way of their happiness.

He told her what had transpired and she smiled happily. There was scarcely time to discuss his visit as they immediately arrived at the gates to their new home.

'Oh my, it has a drive, formal gardens and are those deer grazing on the grass?'

'They are indeed. We cannot see the house yet as it stands in a dip below these trees that line the drive.'

He urged the horse into a trot, eager to see what Bagshot Hall itself was like. His hands were shaking when he drew rein.

'No wonder it's called a hall, sweetheart. It's far bigger than I'd anticipated. It must have half a dozen bedchambers as well as rooms in the attic. It can't be more than fifty years old.'

She clutched his arm. 'How can we possibly afford the rent for something as magnificent?'

'I neglected to tell you that Richard has given us this place as our wedding gift. It has two farms on the estate and is self-sufficient.'

For once she was speechless. A groom was at the horse's head and he jumped down and then lifted her from the high seat.

The front door opened as they ran hand in hand up the scrubbed stone steps. He picked her up and carried her over the threshold, then, ignoring the assembled staff waiting to greet them, he bounded up the stairs and shouldered his way through the nearest door.

Fortunately he'd selected the entrance to the master suite and there was a large bed awaiting them. There was no need to go slowly — she was as eager as he to consummate the union. After all, this wasn't the first time they'd made love and it certainly wouldn't be the last.

★ ★ ★

Mr O'Riley's fears that he was infertile proved baseless and there were four babies born the following year. The Duke of Denchester and his duchess had a fine son in April. Lady Sarah and Mr Marchand produced a beautiful daughter in May and Mr and Mrs O'Riley had both a daughter and a son in July.

Please return/renew this item by the
last date shown to avoid a charge.
Books may also be renewed by phone
and Internet. May not be renewed if
required by another reader.

BARNET
LONDON BOROUGH

K124